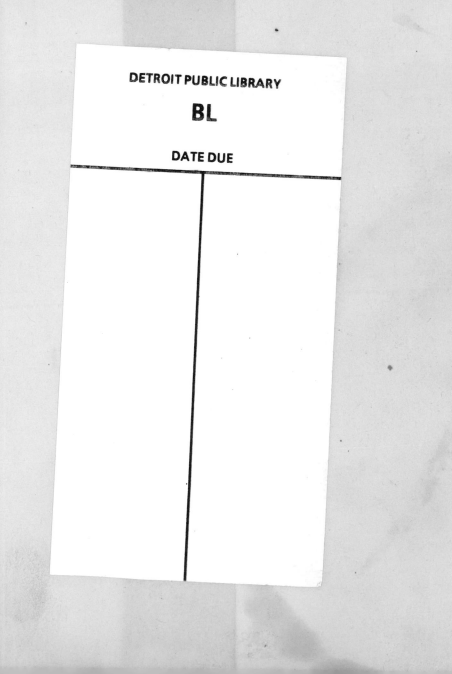

ALSO BY WILLIAM M. GREEN

The Salisbury Manuscript
Avery's Fortune
Spencer's Bag

SEE HOW THEY RUN

by WILLIAM M. GREEN

THE BOBBS-MERRILL COMPANY, INC.
Indianapolis · New York

c. 2

S

Designed by Christopher Simon, Simon-Erikson Associates
Manufactured in the United States of America

First printing

Library of Congress Cataloging in Publication Data

Green, William M
    See how they run.

    I. Title.
PZ4.G79814Ki   [PS3557.R3757]   813'.5'4   75-8639
ISBN 0-672-52163-6

For Jo Stewart

Chapter 1

He was a massive man, with the ponderous face and mottled mane of an aging lion and the florid complexion of the hypertense. For thirty years he had held power by the force of his authority. Now all he had left was his cunning.

He grunted, like a man sated after a good meal, as he squared up the sheaf of papers and photos and placed the tiny cassette of corroborating audio tape on top.

Sewell Crockett had begun this covert and nocturnal enterprise long ago as a diversion, just as some men take up stamp collecting. For a quarter of a century he had gathered, collated, and updated fragments of information about the most private lives of public people, friends and enemies alike. Few men who amounted to anything had nothing to hide, and nobody knew it better than he. In more carefree days it had been an amusing pastime. As some people would drop names, Crockett would drop incidents, discreetly, and only to the individuals directly involved; he was not a gossip. If he was guilty of voyeurism, he considered it a minor vice, one he shared with most of humanity. He was, of course, equipped to indulge in it on a scale undreamed of by most men, having at his command the facilities of the Domestic Security Agency. The DSA was his baby, his fiefdom, his life. He had no family and practically no outside interests.

In the halcyon years of his tenure they had left him alone to do his work; above politics, beyond reproach, he had hammered the agency into an awesomely effective instrument for intelligence gathering and law enforcement. It was the envy of the Johnny-come-lately firms that had mushroomed redundantly in the gloom of the cold war years. It was envy, he was sure, that had led to his harassment in recent years. If a man had something worthwhile, he could count on somebody else's trying to take it away. The predatory instinct was basic to human nature. If it didn't exist, there would be no need for agencies like his.

Two years ago, in his seventy-first year, he had suffered a small stroke, a vascular accident so minor that he had been away from his office for only a week and had succeeded in persuading his doctor to treat him at home. But the vultures had got wind of it. Interpreting his temporary indisposition as a sign of weakness, they had begun circling. Congressional committees, operating under pressure from naive reformers, wanted to dismember him. The mob syndicates, funding dummy social-consciousness groups, wanted to dissolve him. The directors of rival firms wanted to absorb him or swallow him up whole. Under this assault the nocturnal pastime that he had begun as a diversion became his means of survival.

2

With his back to the wall, he resorted to his files, and though he never intended that they would be made public, he let his adversaries sweat out the threat that they might be. The threat was sufficient to make them think twice before attempting to strike at him. It was the political equivalent of a nuclear stand-off.

Crockett chortled as he recalled a meeting with the President less than a month ago. The President wasn't a bad sort: a bit lacking in color, cloyingly pious, but an efficient caretaker and a stolid defender of the status quo. He and Crockett had always gotten along.

At that meeting the President had seemed ill at ease, as he always did when faced with an unpleasant duty. He coughed and fidgeted and tapped at the buttons on his telephone. He expressed his heartfelt gratitude, and the nation's, for Crockett's extraordinary record of service. He voiced his concern over the scarcity of men of Crockett's caliber. He wondered where, when the time came, he would ever find an individual of Crockett's singular capacities and capabilities to assume the directorship of the DSA. Finally, he bemoaned the fact that the time might already be at hand. In this way he backed into a recommendation that Crockett seriously consider a well-earned and honorable retirement. Perhaps a medal could be struck . . . he was almost apologetic. It was, he explained, an election year, and Crockett had become an issue.

Never one to be taken by surprise, Crockett had respectfully replied that, since it was an election year, he had prepared, for the President's consideration, a copy of the dossier he had assembled on that wholesome man's extramarital activities, 1959–1967 inclusive. He opened his briefcase and offered the file.

3

The President was a speed reader. He considered, coughed, and arrived on the spot at one of the pragmatic decisions which were the hallmark of his administration. Crockett and the President had shaken hands like gentlemen; as far as the White House was concerned, the issue was closed. "I hope," the President had said pointedly, "that you are aware that I have no control over the campaign policies of my opposition."

Crockett was aware, and he felt that the work he had completed tonight would ensure that the issue of his retirement would not be raised by either side. To this end he had arranged back-to-back appointments with the principals for the next day.

He pawed a Camel out of the box on his desk and fitted it into a filtered holder with edemic fingers that trembled noticeably. The filtered holder was a concession to the whim of his doctor who had ordered him to give up smoking entirely. He didn't smoke in public anymore. He didn't want his hands up around his face where the tremor would be a highly visible embarrassment, lending credence to the arguments of certain humanitarian congressional leaders who pleaded for his removal on the grounds that he was growing senile—directly contradicting, in his eyes, the braying of the jackass reformers who claimed he was an iron-fisted despot who possessed too much power for an unelected official. What the politicos wanted, what they always wanted, was a piece of the action, and they were willing to sacrifice a professional like him in favor of an amateur to get it. Well, to hell with them all. This was an election year, and before they made a sacrificial goat of him he would damn well kick their balls off.

He lit the cigarette and sucked in a lungful of smoke. Then

4

he laid it down across the ashtray and stood up and stretched, his bulk dwarfing the functional steel desk. He was momentarily overcome by a spell of lightheadedness and shook it off, attributing it to long hours of close work in the bunkerlike study. He flicked on the intercom to tell Tobin, his aide, to start mixing his nightcap, but he couldn't manage to bring the words to his mouth. He saw a lightning flash out of the corner of his eye and knew that was impossible, since his study was in the windowless concrete basement of his home. He closed his eyes and saw more flashes, an electrical storm building inside his head, hissing and popping sounds inside his ears. He opened his eyes and could barely see the room for the flashes, barely see the safe in the opposite wall. Suddenly everything stopped, as if a switch had been thrown inside his skull, and he was engulfed in terrifying silence. This was worse than the last one, much worse. He groped for the precious papers on his desk.

Through the swirling murk of ebbing consciousness he went plunging across the room, stumbling toward the safe which was anchored into a three-foot concrete cube in the opposite wall, the sheaf of papers outthrust in his hand, as if the length of his arm might make a difference. He looked, for a moment, like a tipsy commuter, who had stayed too late and drunk too long, pursuing the last train home as it drew away from the station. He didn't make it. He went crashing into the wall, stumbled back, and dropped to the floor a yard short of his goal. The papers hovered above him for a moment, doing graceful chandelles in the updraft from the ventilator duct. Then they followed him down, settling on his shoulders and around his head on the carpet like falling leaves.

5

Chapter

2

Tobin heard the crash over the intercom and came running. He spun the lock on the armor-plated door that separated the main floor of the house from the basement study. He found Crockett sprawled like a fallen oak, face down on the carpet, the papers scattered around him. Tobin felt his strength draining, as if a tap had been opened somewhere in his gut.

Gingerly he rolled Crockett over onto his back and determined that he was alive, just barely. His eyes were open, but he was unable to acknowledge Tobin's presence. There was no blood, no sign of a wound. There wouldn't be. No intruder could have penetrated Crockett's basement fortress.

Tobin knew what must have happened. Another incidence of what the doctors like to call a vascular accident. Crockett's calcifying arteries had been making warning signals ever since the last one. Crockett knew it, his physician knew it, Tobin knew it. They were the only ones. Crockett had refused hospitalization and some necessary treatment for fear that the news would get out and then the door would be open for the scavengers to move in and pick his bones clean. Power was the name of the game.

Tobin wasn't hungry in that way. He was aware that in most circles he was considered less than a man because of his less than manly appetite. But because of this failing, if it was to be considered a failing, Crockett trusted him as he trusted no one else. He was, in a small way, part of Crockett's greatness, and for Tobin that was enough.

He knelt over the massive, inert form and called, "Sewell? Can you hear me, Sewell?" hopelessly searching for guidance. But none was forthcoming. Not so much as a movement of the head, not a blink of the eyes.

He had no choice. He had to do for Sewell Crockett what Crockett had defiantly refused to do for himself. He had to call for help, even at the risk of letting the world and Crockett's enemies know what Crockett had almost managed to make them forget . . . that Sewell Crockett was mortal.

"God forgive me," he muttered, though it was uncertain to which deity he was addressing himself: the one in heaven or the one lying in ruins on the floor.

He went to the desk, picked up the phone and called an ambulance, speaking so softly—as if Crockett could hear him—that they had to ask him twice to repeat the address. Having completed the call, he knelt again, carefully gathered up the scattered papers and the tape cassette and held them out so that Crockett could see that he was taking care of things—as if Crockett could see.

When he rose to return the file to the safe, his heart almost stopped. The safe was locked, and only Crockett knew the combination. He went to the desk and took a large white 8x10 envelope from Crockett's box of personal stationery. He slipped the papers and the cassette into the envelope and tucked the envelope inside his shirt. He would have to decide what to do with it later. It was a decision he was ill-equipped to make. Maybe in the hospital Dr. Russell could bring Crockett around, and Crockett could tell him what to do with the papers. Until then it would be like carrying a fused bomb against his chest.

Then he remembered: he had forgotten to notify Dr. Russell. The ambulance would come and take Crockett away and deliver him into the hands of some emergency room novice.

Panicky, he went to the phone again and dialed Dr. Russell's number. The red warning light began to flash on the desk. The security sound system hidden in the driveway picked up the whoosh of tires, the squeal of brakes, the thunk of heavy automobile doors. The ambulance had arrived.

Chapter 3

"Has he ever had one of these before?" the intern asked as the ambulance careened out of the driveway and down Q Street. The siren began its wail.

"One of what?" Tobin asked. He was sitting on the bench in the back of the ambulance, staring down at Crockett's stone-still figure.

"Stroke," the intern muttered offhandedly as he finished strapping the oxygen mask over Crockett's expressionless face.

Tobin knew that's what it must have been, but the word sent a shock wave jolting through his system and left him numb. "Once. But he never passed out like this," Tobin answered weakly.

The intern snapped his stethoscope into place on his ears, slipped the diaphragm under Crockett's shirt, and listened.

Tobin wondered if the intern realized who his patient was. Well, he'd know

9

soon enough when they got to the hospital and signed in, and it wouldn't be long after that before the whole world would know. Probably knew already. Someone in the neighborhood must have seen the ambulance in Crockett's driveway. The wires must be humming. Tobin wished he hadn't called the ambulance. He had panicked. He should have called Dr. Russell first. There might have been a way to do it more quietly.

The ambulance was speeding at full tilt now down the deserted straightaway of Wisconsin Avenue, trailing the sound of its siren like a banner.

"Is he going to be all right?" Tobin asked the intern apprehensively.

"Are you family?" the intern asked in reply as he shone his penlight into Crockett's right eye.

Tobin might have replied, "I'm his friend, his only friend," but he simply said, "I work for him."

The intern grunted and beamed the light into Crockett's left eye.

"Do you know where to reach his family?" the intern asked.

"He doesn't have any family," Tobin answered. "Is he going to die?" If he was Crockett's only friend, Crockett was his only reason for being. He was like the pilot fish that would be lost without its shark.

The intern shrugged as he wound the band of a sphygmomanometer around Crockett's limp arm. He squeezed the rubber bulb a few times and watched the rise and fall of the column of mercury. "He seems to be holding his own. He might make it. He might be walking around in a week or two. He might be a vegetable for the rest of his life."

Tobin felt the envelope under his shirt like a knife against

10

his belly. What right had he to assume custodianship of such awesome material? "How long before you know?" Tobin asked.

The intern looked at Tobin for the first time. His eyes were tired, careworn beyond his years. His voice was almost a sigh. "It's a waiting game, Mr. —?"

"Tobin."

The intern nodded. "Mr. Tobin. Yeah. With this kind of thing it's a waiting game."

As the ambulance took the corner into Twenty-fourth Street, Tobin caught a glimpse of the hospital up ahead. He twisted around on the bench to get a better look, and again felt the knife edge of the envelope against his belly. He shuddered.

He had served Crockett with unswerving loyalty for half a lifetime—more than served him: revered him. It had cost him first the respect and then the love of his wife. It had cost him the estrangement of his son. Only his daughter, it seemed, had been capable of understanding.

Now, gratuitous circumstance had made him steward of the fortunes of the man he had served. The burden was his because there was no one else to whom it could be entrusted. But no one knew better than he how inadequate he was to cope with such responsibility.

When the ambulance arrived at the hospital, Dr. Russell was waiting. He supervised Crockett's transfer from the ambulance to a stretcher trolley and rolled him away, like a piece of broken machinery, to intensive care.

Through the glass-paneled doors Tobin saw the first press car drive up. By tomorrow morning everyone would know. The vultures would start descending.

11

Chapter 4

Tobin left the hospital by a side door and began walking in the general direction of home, unmindful of the dank night air, ignoring the importuning horns of passing cabs.

Nearly an hour later he found himself on a run-down stretch of Pennsylvania Avenue, all but abandoned at this late hour. He was feeling the cold in his bones now. The red neon sign of an all-night Rexall glowed invitingly and he went inside. The place was empty, except for a counterman, laconically cleaning the orange juice machine, and a pharmacist reading a newspaper.

"Chilly out there tonight . . . " the counterman said. He wanted to talk. Tobin didn't. He ordered a cup of coffee and then carried it from the counter to one of the booths against the opposite wall. He slid into the booth, pulled the little cap off the thimble-sized plastic cream container and dumped the cream into the inky coffee. The cream curdled. It must have been sitting near one of the heating units since morning. He skimmed the cheesy film off the top with his spoon and poured in some sugar.

He stirred the brew slowly, staring down at the little whirlpool his rotating spoon was creating, trying to decide, as he had tried to decide during his long walk from the hospital, what to do with the envelope he had tucked away under his shirt. He reached in and took the envelope out and sat staring at it, and emitted a sound halfway between a sigh and a groan. He wondered if he had any right to examine what surely must be most sensitive material, yet he felt he had to know what he was handling before he could come to a decision as to its proper disposition. He watched his fingers, as if they belonged to someone else, lift the flap and draw the sheets of paper out. The pages were in no proper order, having been stuffed into the envelope haphazardly as he had picked them up off the floor. The blocked paragraphs, headed with the name of a speaker, looked like the transcript of a meeting: the actual voices doubtlessly recorded on the accompanying tape cassette. As he shuffled the pages, putting them in order, he couldn't help noticing a name that kept appearing at the tops of most of the paragraphs. Senator John Ashley was present and doing a good deal of the talking. Albert Moore, the secretary of the treasury, was present, too. There were three or four other names Tobin didn't recognize. One of the pages, which was obviously meant to be the first page, cleared up the identities of the others and outlined the thrust of the ensuing detailed transcript. This first page was headed: "Transcript of the Meeting called by Senator John Ashley to Discuss the

Feasibility of Blocking the Bank Accounts and Other Holdings of Certain Members of the Association of Oil Producing and Exporting Countries.

"The meeting was called by Senator Ashley and held aboard the yacht *Dolphin* belonging to Allen Montgomery, chairman of the board of the Federal National Bank. Present, in addition to Senator Ashley and Mr. Montgomery, were Albert Moore, secretary of the treasury, Wayne Sommers, chairman of the SEC, Frederick Turner of the Commercial Industrial Bank, and Edward Day of the United Federated Banking Corporation."

Tobin read no further. He slipped the papers back into the envelope and tucked the envelope inside his shirt. The most powerful senator on the Hill, the secretary of the treasury, the chairman of the SEC, and the heads of three of the largest banks in the country were considering freezing the bank accounts and investments of a selected group of foreign nations. Whatever conclusions were drawn from that meeting, the fact that such a proposal was in the air could bring about an economic earthquake if word ever got out.

Tobin hurried from the drugstore and took the first cab that came along back to Crockett's house.

As Tobin got out of the cab, he could hear a phone ringing with the strident urgency that phones seem to have when they go unanswered in an empty house. He began to run, wondering if it might be a call from Dr. Russell at the hospital. He got through the door and picked up the extension in the foyer in time to hear the line go dead. He dialed information and got the number of the hospital, then hung up the phone so that he could redial. The ringing began

14

again. He snatched up the receiver and pressed it to his ear. "Crockett residence. Tobin here."

"Tobin. This is General Dahlgren." The general hardly had to identify himself. Tobin, like most other Americans, would have recognized the clipped parade-ground diction anywhere. That voice and the Mount Rushmore face and the close-cropped gunmetal-gray hair had been getting maximum TV exposure lately. A high-powered campaign was being mounted to groom the one-time war hero and recently retired chairman of the Joint Chiefs of Staff for a shot at the presidency in the upcoming election. Dahlgren was potentially the most formidable candidate to come along since Eisenhower, a cinch to swamp the competent but colorless incumbent. But for all his charisma, Dahlgren was no Eisenhower. He lacked Eisenhower's basic integrity and deep-seated respect for democratic processes. If he could be compared to any military figure of the recent past, it would have to be to Patton.

"I've been ringing the bells off that phone of yours, Tobin." He made it sound like a reprimand. "What seems to be wrong with our friend Crockett?" Tobin hadn't seen Dahlgren's name in the transcript of the meeting on the banker's yacht. But he knew that Crockett must have something on General Dahlgren, because the general wasn't calling at half-past one in the morning out of genuine concern for Crockett's health.

"Just an indisposition, sir," Tobin lied. "He'll be back at his desk in no time at all."

"Don't bullshit me, Tobin. The press briefing at the hospital called it a vascular accident."

"I didn't know about the briefing, sir. I've been out . . . ."

"I'll bet you have. Now you damn well better level with me, Tobin. I'm not some newspaper punk."

"I can't tell you any more, general." Then he added, pointedly, "If you're concerned about your appointment with Mr. Crockett tomorrow . . . "

"Who the hell said anything about an appointment?" Dahlgren exploded.

"Mr. Crockett's files are well secured, and they'll stay that way until Mr. Crockett is back at his desk."

"I want you to inform me, personally, you hear, any time of day or night of any change in status. I don't forget my friends, Tobin, or my enemies." Dahlgren hung up.

Tobin dropped the receiver back into its cradle, happily astonished by the effectiveness of his performance. He hadn't known he had it in him. He had no idea whether or not Crockett had assembled a file on Dahlgren. But he was aware that Crockett had set up an appointment to see Dahlgren in the morning, and he had considered that, coupled with the general's distress, significant. He had let the general know that Sewell Crockett, though temporarily incapacitated, was still very much a force to be reckoned with.

The telephone rang again. He hesitated before picking it up, wondering if it would be Dahlgren again. Perhaps it had been a mistake on his part to leave the general with the impression that he knew where the files were.

The call was from Steve Kiley, the President's appointments secretary, inquiring on behalf of the President about the state of Mr. Crockett's health. He, like the general, had been calling for hours. Tobin wondered how many calls had been made this night. Kiley was less overbearing and far more diplomatic in his approach than the general was, but if his prime concern was for Crockett's physical condition, he could have gotten a more complete report from Crockett's doctor. Tobin assured him, as he had assured the general, that Crockett's files were secure.

When the phone rang again, a moment later, it was Senator Ashley, who, in addition to his secret foray into the nether regions of international banking, was publicly leading a fight on the Hill to force Crockett into retirement. Welcome to the club, Tobin thought as he offered the senator the same pointed assurances he had given to the general and to Kiley. Then, before the phone could ring again, he went into Miss Yarborough's empty reception room and pulled all the plugs on the switchboard.

He felt that he had done well, so far. He didn't want to press his luck. He was emotionally exhausted. His head weighed a ton. And he still didn't know what to do about the envelope he was carrying. Leaning heavily on the bannister, battling a hammering headache, he trudged up to his room on the second floor.

He took two aspirins and washed them down with bourbon, and sat down in a comfortable chair to wait until his head stopped pounding and he could think again. He slipped off, obliviously, into sleep, his hand still curled around the whiskey glass, the glass resting on the arm of his chair. The ice cubes turned to water; the water grew lukewarm in the bottom of the glass. Eventually he moved his hand, and the glass fell, almost soundlessly, onto the carpeted floor; it didn't wake him. The dull thump of a muffled explosion did, a kind of earth shock, more felt than heard, coming from somewhere beneath the house.

He blinked his eyes open, momentarily confused, trying to recall when he had fallen asleep, trying to identify the sensation that had wakened him. Then he knew. He lurched out of the chair and ran for the stairs, aware even as he ran that he would be too late.

He was halfway down the stairs to the main floor of the house when he heard the second report from the basement, the one which he knew would follow inevitably upon the opening of the door to the safe.

The door to the basement was half open. He remembered now that he had gone upstairs without resealing it. The acrid smell of cordite was in the air. The safe door was wide open, hanging slightly askew, its hinges ruptured by the initial charge. He didn't see the man at first, but he knew he would have to be somewhere in the room. Then he saw his feet, propped up on the desk, almost casually. Tobin approached the desk cautiously, following with his eyes the line from the intruder's feet to his thighs to where his hips rested on the floor. The hips made a forty-five-degree angle with the torso, which lay flat on its back, arms outflung ·as if nailed to an invisible cross. There wasn't a mark on the man from his feet to his neck. But there was a puddle of blood where the top of his head should have been, and part of his skull was lying a yard or so away against the wall.

Crockett had had his safe rigged with a twelve-gauge shotgun loaded and cocked and wired to go off if the door was opened in any way but the one prescribed by the manufacturer. The double-barreled blast had caught the man full in the face and thrown him back halfway across the room.

Tobin knelt and fished the man's wallet out of his breast pocket, and found in it half a dozen driver's licenses and credit cards made out in as many names. There was also an ID card that Tobin recognized as authentic and which identified the intruder as a special projects operative in Crockett's own Domestic Security Agency.

Tobin cleaned the wallet of fingerprints and slipped it back into the man's pocket, but he kept the ID card. When—if—Crockett came out of the hospital he would want to know who had tried to take advantage of his absence.

Tobin crossed back to the blown safe to make sure there was nothing of value inside, not that he expected that there would be. He knew for a fact that Crockett kept the bulk of his private intelligence locked up pseudonymously in bank vaults scattered all over the Washington area. Crockett used the basement safe only for overnight storage of the file he was currently assembling, and Tobin had that one in the envelope in his room upstairs. So he was surprised to find, tucked away in the back of the safe under the protective muzzle of the shotgun, a manila folder and, bound together by a rubber band, five tiny gray envelopes.

Gingerly he removed the material from the safe and took it over to the desk, trying to ignore the upraised shoes of the intruder. He didn't have to examine the manila folder; its contents were immediately and astonishingly apparent. The name "Dahlgren" was clearly lettered on the tab. The tiny gray envelopes puzzled him. He slipped one of them out of the elastic binding. He undid the string that held the flap down and upended the envelope over his open palm. A small, flat metal key dropped into his hand, a simple-looking key with a tiny cardboard disc tied to its handle. There was an initial printed on the disc in India ink. There was no other mark of identification. Tobin knew what it must be. He passed the back of his hand across his forehead, as if he could erase his dilemma. His hand began to tremble. He laid the key down on the desk. He tried not to look at the feet of the dead man propped up across from him. One by one he opened the other envelopes and laid their contents out on the desk. Five keys, all vaguely similar in appearance, except for a different initial on each cardboard tag and a variance in the configuration of the teeth.

Tobin scooped up the keys and closed his fist tightly around them. He could feel them cutting into the palm of his hand. He stared at the broken safe. There was no way he could lock it again. If the contents of the papers he had undertaken to protect were volatile, they at least pertained only to a circumscribed group of men. The keys in his hand could unlock enough explosive material to sink the whole ship of state.

The dead man behind him had come in search of a single file. He might have been sent by Dahlgren, Ashley, the President, anyone.

Had he found the keys . . .

The consequences were too overwhelming to contemplate. Crockett, for all his precautions, had simply failed to consider, or refused to consider, the possibility that one day he might be totally incapacitated.

Tobin left the basement study. He felt weak and lightheaded. He wondered if he would have the strength to climb the stairs back to his room. He fell onto his bed and lay there, gasping, trying to force his reluctant mind to work.

The dead man in the study was no problem. He could leave that to the daytime staff. They would find the body in the morning and notify the police of an aborted break-in. He, Tobin, would be long gone by then. He couldn't remain in the house with the papers and the keys that had just come into his possession. He would have to decide what to do with them, but first he would have to get out. The break-in a few minutes ago was only the beginning. In a sense the house would be under siege. Crockett's disability had opened the floodgates, and as long as his condition remained in doubt, nothing in the building would be secure.

Tobin forced himself to get off the bed. Like a paralytic willing himself to undertake the agonizing labors of rehabilitation, he forced himself to function. He slipped the contents of the Dahlgren file into the 8x10 envelope that already contained the Ashley transcript. He cut a shirt cardboard down to size so that it too would fit into the envelope. One by one he taped the keys to the cardboard, then slipped the cardboard into the envelope, sealed it carefully, and reinforced the seal and all the seams with tape.

He was still at a loss over what to do with the envelope; that would take the kind of thought he was incapable of tonight. He would have to decide on a place where it would be safe, a place separate from his person, for surely they would come after him. It would have to be some place not generally associated with either Crockett or himself, some place that none of the bloodhounds would consider, some place from which he could retrieve it for Crockett if Crockett survived, or destroy it if Crockett was no longer able to exercise control. And in the event that neither he nor Crockett was capable of retrieving or destroying it, he would have to decide on someone he could trust to do that job for him.

His head felt as if it were being crushed in a vise. He gulped two more aspirins. Then he went to the closet where he kept his traveling gear. He bypassed his two expensive new suitcases, hoping that their presence in the closet might camouflage for a little while the fact of his flight. In the back of the closet, among old storage cartons, he found what he

21

was looking for, an ancient scuffed leather bag that he hadn't used in years. No one on the daytime staff was even aware of its existence.

He opened it and found that it still contained a few artifacts left over from long-ago journeys: ossifying tooth-paste and shaving cream tubes, faded ticket stubs, souvenir postcards and tourist folders from places he had been in what seemed like another life.

He left these things undisturbed and packed around them just one extra shirt, one set of underclothes, socks, an extra pair of trousers, a sweater. When he was through, his dresser drawers and closets still looked full and undisturbed. He left his razor and toothbrush behind; he could pick up toilet articles along the way as he needed them. He thought about packing the envelope into the suitcase and decided against it, feeling that it would be better to keep it on his person, the quicker to dump it, scatter it, destroy it if necessary.

He picked up the suitcase and stepped out into the upstairs hall, quietly closing his bedroom door behind him. He stood and listened for a moment, sensing other move-ment in the house. He heard ratlike rustling sounds coming from the basement study, and then a gasped expletive. Another break-in—already—and the new intruder had just discovered the body of his predecessor.

Tobin tiptoed along the corridor to the back stairway, quietly descended and left the house by way of the kitchen.

Chapter 5

The blue norther had come roaring in during the night, rattling the bedroom windows as they tried to sleep; a marauding nightrider, demanding entry, laying siege, surrounding the white clapboard house with a chill so palpable that the walls began to radiate the cold.

They molded their bodies to each other and clung together for warmth under the double layer of woolen blankets. But sleep was out of the question. It was always out of the question when they lay together like that. It was hardly even worthwhile this night. They had to be up at six to get Jim to the airport for the 8:30 flight out.

As the temperature inside the house plummeted, they kept each other warm in the most timeless of ways, neither noticing nor caring when the blankets slid off the bed.

When the warmth generated by their

23

lovemaking was spent, they both began to shiver. Jim rolled across her and out of bed. The old floor creaked like a ship in heavy seas. "Hey! Where do you think you're going?" she complained teasingly. "This isn't a ten-dollar-an-hour joint." The words were no sooner out than she regretted them. They had formed in her mind as a joke, but they played unsettlingly on her ears, articulating something that had been troubling her for some weeks now. Lately she had begun to feel a little like a whore, going through the motions, counterfeiting the outward signs of a love that she was no longer sure of. She was still fond of him at times, and she still took pleasure in the touch of his body. But love? Certainly nothing like what she had felt when they had begun to share the house a year and a half ago. Certainly nothing deep or lasting enough to sustain a lifelong relationship, which was what he now wanted.

He picked up one of the blankets that had fallen on the floor, shook it out, and tucked it around her. Considerate. But she wondered if his consideration hadn't taken on a ritual aspect, compensating for a similar loss of spontaneity. Yet he had become more insistent lately that they legitimatize their relationship; petrify would be a better word. She wondered if his importunings weren't a little less than sincere, now that he had entered into the career phase of his life. She suspected that he had subconsciously begun to cast her in a wifely role subordinate to and supportive of his own role as a rising young man in the business world. She dreaded becoming an ornament to be worn on his arm at corporate functions, a hostess, a mother of sons and heirs. She wondered if it was fair of her to keep from him the news that he was already on his way to being a father.

She watched him hopping from foot to foot to keep his

24

toes from freezing to the floor while he wrapped the second blanket around himself Indian style. He looked just like the boy she had once loved with boundless certainty.

They had met just eighteen months ago on the campus of Southwestern Tech. He had been a senior in the School of Petroleum Engineering. She had just started her course of studies in anthropology. There were specialized areas in which their fields had crossed. The chemistry had been just right; it still was, in a narrowly circumscribed way. The campus was still there, just thirty minutes by car from where they were living now. She was still a student. Everything else had changed.

He danced gingerly across the room and picked up a box of matches from the dresser. He hunkered down near the gas heater and struck a light. There was a serpentlike hiss of gas . . . and *whoom*. Bright blue flame erupted from the double row of jets.

"Don't you think an up-and-coming young petroleum engineer should at least have an oil burner in the basement . . . just to kind of set an example?"

"Sure do," he replied cheerily. "Soon's we get a house with a basement." He danced out of the room, the house shaking with his heavy step as he went to light the heaters in the kitchen and the bathroom. Well, she thought, he isn't so bad. But he wasn't the problem. The problem was what to do about the kind of life she had. once envisioned for herself. Jim would be leaving in an hour or so for a three-week tour of Guatemala, part of a company team surveying the coastal areas and back country for promising drilling sites. Where would she ever go? Once she had dreamed of digs and discoveries. What would she discover, when she finished her studies . . . that there was no room at a dig for a woman with a child? Of course she could teach. She could take her knowledge and her enthusiasm and transmit them to someone else who could go out into the field.

The house began to shake again as Jim came hopping back to the bedroom. He hit the bed with a shudder. "Brr, this mattress is like ice." She moved over a little so he could share the place she had made warm with her body. He pressed himself against her and spread the blanket over them both.

"Ah. That's better," he murmured.

An hour later when the alarm went off it was still dark outside.

Andrea wiped away the condensation on the kitchen window with the palm of her hand, leaned across the sink and squinted at the thermometer taped to the outside of the glass. There was just enough illumination from the overhead light to make out the red-dyed column of alcohol standing at the twenty-five-degree mark. That was cold, cold for anywhere, but especially damned shuddering cold for Texas. She could hear Jim stomping back and forth in the bedroom, opening and slamming closet doors and dresser drawers as he threw his clothes and gear into the two beat-up bags he traveled with. "You better wear your long johns," she shouted. "It's colder than an actuary's heart out there."

The bacon sizzling in the black cast-iron skillet began to pop and spit. She picked up a fork and turned the slices, then lowered the flame a little. A pungent, mouth-watering aroma of smoked hickory began to permeate the room. "Almost ready?" she yelled.

"Two minutes," Jim shouted back, as he stomped across the narrow passageway between the bedroom and the bathroom. His electric razor began to buzz, as if a nest of wasps had been let loose.

Andrea cracked four eggs in rapid succession, plopped them into a porcelain mixing bowl, added a little milk, and beat them into a cloudy froth.

She turned the flame off under the skillet and set the bacon out to drain on a paper towel. She clicked the radio on to see if she could get a weather forecast. The roads should be all right, as long as it wasn't drizzling anywhere.

She was scraping the eggs out of the pan onto a large serving plate when she half-heard the name Crockett. She stopped what she was doing and listened, but she'd already missed a connective sentence. ". . . his condition has been described as guarded. Now, turning to the local news, the Hagerston Chamber of Commerce yesterday issued a declaration . . . "

Andrea spun the dial through the frequencies, into and out of a cacophony of guitar bleats, trumpet blasts, rock shrieks, and bluegrass wails, but found no more news summaries.

When Jim came in she was looking thoughtful. "Sewell Crockett's in the hospital," she said.

"I'll bet that's made the day for a lot of folks in Washington."

"Not for my dad."

"You want to phone him?"

"It's too early now. He probably had a rough night. I'll call him when I get back from school. Now let's eat up and get out of here or you'll miss your plane."

They had some trouble getting the car started. Jim leaped out and yanked open the hood, cursing and laying blame, as was his habit when things didn't go according to plan.

"Did you put in antifreeze?"

"Who would think of antifreeze in Texas?"

"Lucky the engine block's not cracked." The sun had dragged itself up onto the wintry wall of the horizon, glowing weakly, like a fifteen-watt bulb behind a dirty windowpane. He pumped gas into the carburetor manually, and they got the car going.

Jim's farewell words to her at the airport were: "You won't forget the antifreeze, now, will you?" She was so mad she stalled the engine as she started to drive away.

After school she stopped at a service station and had antifreeze put in. "Lucky you didn't crack your block last night, little lady."

"So I've been told." While the pump jockey drained and refilled her radiator, she walked over to the supermarket and bought a week's assortment of frozen dinners. When she got home, it was 5:30, the sun had set, and the house was freezing again.

She kept her coat on while she went from room to room, lighting the gas heaters. Then she slipped a Chicken Steak Dinner into the oven, set the timer for forty-five minutes, and went to call her father.

She dialed the number of the private phone in her father's room in Crockett's house and got no answer. She dialed the number of the house proper and got no answer either. She thought that was damned strange. But it didn't worry her. Her father might have been out, might have been visiting Crockett at the hospital. And, since it was past six o'clock in Washington, Crockett's personal secretary would have left for the day . . . if she had come in at all.

The next morning she stopped off at the post office on her way to class and picked up the mail. There was a letter from him.

Dear Andrea,

By the time you get this, the news will be out regarding Mr. Crockett's illness. I know you will pray for his speedy recovery, as I do. In the meantime I have been forced to take it upon myself to protect certain documents of his. I know I'm not up to such a responsibility, but I don't know where else to turn.

These documents were left exposed when he was suddenly taken ill. If they should fall into the wrong hands, the consequences would be very grave, for him if he recovers, for all of us if he should not. I hate to think what would happen if they should ever come into public view.

I have sent these documents to a place where I think they will be safe. Should Mr. Crockett live, as we pray he will, I will return the documents to him. Should the good Lord see fit to take him, I will destroy the documents. That is my plan as it stands now.

But I am getting on, just like Mr. Crockett, and who knows what infirmities each passing day may bring. And there may be certain parties who will try to stop me. So now I must ask you for the promise of a favor which I hope sincerely you will never have to do, but there is no one else that I can truly trust.

Should I be unable to take the documents from their safekeeping place, when the time comes, and return them to Mr. Crockett, or destroy them as the situation calls for, I ask you to do it for me.

She reread the last paragraph and shuddered, and then realized she was standing in the post office and there were people watching. She folded the letter, slipped it back into the envelope, and hurried out to the car. There she began reading again, picking up at the point where she had stopped.

I would not dream of placing you in danger, not even for this. And I feel safe in the conviction that no harm will come to you. Your way of life is too far removed from our way of life. The only inconvenience you will have to suffer is that of travel. You will have to go to the safekeeping place, claim the envelope containing the documents, which it will be your right to do, and burn the envelope without opening it. If the time should come, I will send you a message which I know you will understand. It will tell you where to go. Should you receive it, I know you will behave in accordance with my wishes.

You have always been a good and trustworthy daughter, and I have not been the world's best father. But there has always been a feeling of family between us. I only wish your brother had turned out to be the kind of man who could have been trusted with this confidence. Then I could have turned to him, as the man in the family, and not burdened you. But there is no use crying over spilt milk, now, is there?

Please destroy this letter after you have read it, and speak of it to no one . . . With all my love . . .

She didn't go to class that day. She hit the starter, turned the car around, and sped back toward the house. A little more than halfway there, she pulled the car over onto the shoulder, took out the letter and read it again. She wondered if Crockett's collapse might have precipitated an emotional breakdown in her father; he had been tied to Crockett for so much of his life. Alienation. Paranoia. If Crockett went, Tobin's whole reason for being went with him.

She jammed her foot down on the accelerator, climbed back onto the road, fishtailed, corrected, and headed for home, doing seventy flat-out.

This time Crockett's secretary answered the phone. She sounded harassed. No, she was sorry to say, Mr. Tobin was not in. No, he was not visiting Mr. Crockett. He had not been seen all day. She wished she knew where he was. Among the people hovering about, an unconscionable number seemed more concerned with Mr. Tobin's whereabouts than with Mr. Crockett's health. Yes, grudgingly, wearily, she would ask Mr. Tobin, when he returned, to contact his daughter.

Chapter 6

Tobin was sitting on a flaking wooden stool in the third-floor loft of an abandoned cast-iron building on Mercer Street in New York. The interior of the building was chokingly redolent of generations of stray cats and homeless men. The beat-up old stool was the only piece of furniture in the cavernous room. He could have sworn that it was one of a pair of stools that he and Crockett had brought there, along with a wooden table and an army cot, back in 1938 when they were both newly fledged agents working a round-the-clock surveillance of a counterfeiting operation across the street.

The table, the other stool, and the cot were gone now, of course, stolen or broken up for firewood by one or more of the countless numbers of derelicts who must have found shelter in the corroding old structure during the intervening years. The building had been abandoned even when Crockett and Tobin had taken up their vigil.

This time Tobin had no company, except for the nine-dollar transistor radio he had bought at the railroad station before leaving Washington. He used the broad flat side of his closed suitcase as a table, and a sleeping bag for a cot. For light he had a battery-powered miner's lamp that he had purchased along with the sleeping bag at a surplus goods store on Canal Street a few blocks away.

He was perched on the stool, crouching over the suitcase at his feet, trying to win a game of solitaire when the news came over the radio that Crockett had regained consciousness.

Tobin felt his eyes flooding. Tears of gratitude. Tears of relief. For nine awful days Crockett had lain like a vegetable; a man so powerful, so revered, and, yes, so feared by some. For nine awful days Tobin had borne the terrible and unaccustomed weight of responsibility alone. "Thank God," Tobin muttered. It was over.

For some minutes he remained immobile on the stool, doubled up, his forehead in his hands. Finally, he took out his handkerchief and cleaned up his face. He couldn't let himself cave in now. He had to get word to Crockett that the documents were safe.

Tobin shone the light on his watch. It was almost midnight. He would call Crockett in the morning. His news would be better medicine than anything the doctors could prescribe. Then, depending on Crockett's instructions, he would either claim the envelope or leave it in its safekeeping place until Crockett was ready to receive it. In either case the burden would no longer be his. He could retreat again into the welcome shade of anonymity.

33

He checked the wallet-sized timetable he carried in his pocket and made a mental note. He lit a match to the timetable and let it fall in flames onto the stained floor. He ground the curled ash into powder and spread the powder around with his shoe. Then, for the third time in the nine days since he had left Crockett's house, he packed the battered old suitcase with which he had been traveling and prepared to move out again.

He heard the car drive up and stop in the deserted street outside. He turned out the miner's lamp, though he knew it was already too late; the light must have been seen. He went to the window that faced the street.

The front doors of the car popped open synchronously. The two men got out with the snap and precision of a football squad breaking from a huddle. They came together in front of the car, exchanged a few words, nodded their heads in mutual agreement. Set. Hike. They started toward the building, purposefully, businesslike. Tobin knew the style.

He had misjudged them. The news of Crockett's improved condition, rather than driving them into retreat, had moved them to attack, quickly, before Crockett regained his strength. Despairingly, he realized that, for all his evasive action, his zigzagging and doubling back and changing of base, he had never been out of their sight for very long. It had been a long time since he had been operative. But though they had clung to him like ticks, they were nowhere near their objective. He'd done that part right. The closer they came to him, the farther they were from the file.

He heard footsteps starting up the iron stairway two floors below. Out-of-step. *Ka-lunk, lunk, da-lunk, kalang.* Relaxed. Sure of themselves. No attempt to surprise him. They had

34

come to make a deal. Turn over the documents and go in peace. No hard feelings. Except that he knew they'd never let him go in peace. They couldn't. Because they couldn't be sure whether, by now, he had in his head what was in the files.

He wasn't concerned about that. If he could elude them for just a little while, just long enough to get word to Crockett about the file, it wouldn't matter when they hit him.

He could hear them moving around on the floor below, scraping and shuffling like loft mice, probably using a flashlight, probing for him.

Tobin unzipped the accessories pocket in his suitcase and took out a picture postcard. It was already stamped, addressed, and signed. It was to have been the signal to his daughter telling her where to claim and destroy the envelope. He fumbled for a match, intending to burn the card. With Crockett on the mend, he wouldn't need Andrea's help. He certainly didn't want Crockett's papers destroyed now.

Ka-lang, k-klunk-dalunk, kalunk. They were moving up to his floor. There wasn't time. He blew out the match and stuck the postcard into his coat pocket. He climbed out the window that faced onto the back alley. He left the suitcase where it was. Maybe they'd waste a few minutes looking through it.

He sent a tremor up and down the length of the fire escape with every step he took. But he was sure they couldn't hear. He'd taken care to shut the window behind him. He had charted this escape route, in case he should need it, on the day he had moved into the loft. He unhooked the catch on the ladder that lowered from the first floor to the street, but lost his grip. Falling free, it took just a second and a half for the thing to slide to the sidewalk, screeching hideously all the way. The base of the ladder hit the pavement in the alley with a crash, and a moment later, while Tobin was still scurrying down the rungs, he heard the window above him being thrown open.

He looked up from the alley and saw the first of the two men climbing out onto the fire escape. And then he started to run. He would need every yard of headway he had, because he was sixty years old and he knew he couldn't run very long or very far.

At the end of the block he glanced back and saw the lead man coming out of the alley, and was seen by him as he rounded the corner. He felt that he still could lose them if he could make it to Canal Street, with its people and traffic and a half dozen subway entrances giving onto a maze of platforms and tunnels.

He sprang for the curb. A searing pain shot up his leg as he landed. His ankle had turned in a broken patch in the sidewalk. Arms windmilling, he fought for balance, righted himself, and hobbled on in quick, short, limping strides.

The corner of Broome and Broadway was silent and deserted at this time of night. Two short blocks away, straight down Broadway, he could see shimmering color and light. Canal Street was alive with tourists overflowing from Chinatown across the way. He was breathing hard. His chest felt like it was in irons. He glanced back and didn't see them coming. He couldn't believe they would let him go so easily. Then he heard their ignition kick over and the starting roar of their engine. They were coming after him in the car. How cool. No public spectacle. No chasing through the streets, drawing attention and maybe interference. They'd let him run for as long as he could, and they'd cruise along after him.

When he'd run himself out, they'd be there. They'd pick him up, almost casually. Not if he could reach the subway.

Canal Street was just a half block away now, its traffic boom muted by the hammering all around him, his heart in his chest, his pulse in his ears, his feet on the pavement, and the pistons of the black Plymouth cruising along in low gear about ten yards behind him—just keeping pace.

Faces on the corner were turning to stare as he rushed, limping, toward them, puffing, sparse hair blowing, coat flapping. A madman, a fugitive from the Bowery nearby, teeth bared, lips drawn back in a rictus—a runaway thief.

Gaping, they scurried back out of his way. He didn't see them anymore. All he saw was the haven of the subway entrance across the street. He burst out through the crowd into the street. He didn't see the taxi speeding to beat the light. He didn't even feel it hit him.

Suddenly, unaccountably, he was airborne, tumbling, and the subway entrance was receding into darkness. He hit halfway up the traffic light pole and came thudding down in the midst of the crowd that had just parted to let him through. They backed off even farther now and stood in a half circle around him, paralyzed with shock. The first hands to reach him belonged to the men who had been following in the Plymouth. They shouldered their way through the crowd with an air of authority and knelt over his broken body, ostensibly giving first aid, feeling for pulse beats and fractures, signs of life, all the while thoroughly searching him with such finesse that none of the bystanders in the crowd was aware of what was going on. They found nothing of value. The picture postcard might have been meaningful to someone well briefed on Tobin's past. But it was lying several yards away under the feet of the crowd, having fluttered from his pocket as he tumbled through the air. The frisk took the men from the Plymouth less than two minutes. Then one of them, Larsen, looked up and yelled admonishingly at the crowd, "You gonna stand there all night? Call an ambulance." Half a dozen people ran for the same phone booth in the candy store on the corner.

Larsen left his partner, Shepard, with Tobin and drifted back through the crowd. He left the car parked where it was, for Shepard to use, and ambled along Canal until he came to Lafayette Street, one block east of Broadway.

He turned quickly up Lafayette and strode purposefully north in the general direction of the loft just vacated by Tobin. A half block up from Canal Street the area became deserted again. A cinch to spot a tag, if there was one, though he knew of no reason why there should be. A block from Broome Street and the loft building he checked again. Occupational reflex, born of training and habit, not to be sneered at; the time you let up is the time you get clobbered.

As he crossed the cobblestone roadway on Broome, he heard the ambulance wail floating on the cold dry air up from Canal, buffered to a sigh by the buildings and streets in between. He reentered the loft building and quickly mounted the iron stairs to the third floor.

The area Tobin had been living in was a large, bare rectangle, twenty by at least a hundred feet. Faded, peeling plaster walls, veined with cracks, but no sign that the plaster had been broken open and then patched. You could pretty well do the room at a glance. There was no place he could have hidden anything, except maybe under the floorboards, and a special crew would have to be called in for a search there. There was the suitcase lying on its side on the floor, and the sleeping bag nearby.

He drew on a pair of rubber surgical gloves and began with the suitcase. Five minutes later his search confirmed what his instincts told him he would find. Nothing. A shirt, some socks, some underwear, a pair of trousers, some shiny new shaving equipment, a toothbrush, a cheap pocket-sized transistor radio. Nothing hidden inside the toothpaste tube, the shaving cream can, or the little radio. Nothing in the linings or the pockets. Nothing anywhere. He repacked the suitcase exactly as he had found it, except for the toothpaste tube and shaving cream can, which were totaled. There was nothing in the sleeping bag either, except the lingering odor of a man who had slept inside and sweated a good deal.

Larsen heard a scraping of feet on the iron stairs and wondered what Shepard was doing back here; he was supposed to have stayed with Tobin. The footsteps stopped at the first landing, and Larsen knew it wasn't Shepard. Shepard would have come straight up. He knew there was no watchman. The building was abandoned. They'd had it under surveillance ever since Tobin had moved in thirty-eight hours ago.

Larsen made a quick visual check of the loft; everything was as it had been when he had come in. Then he moved quickly, soundlessly, to the window. It was still open from when they'd gone out after Tobin. He climbed onto the fire escape and slid the window shut. He moved the frame with utmost care, but it was warped and swollen, and it creaked and groaned in its tracks. He hoped that whoever was down on the floor below wouldn't hear. He figured they wouldn't hear. Shepard and he hadn't heard Tobin open the window.

39

They'd only heard the iron ladder crash into the alley below. He glanced down. The ladder was still extended to the pavement. Good.

Larsen flattened himself against the exterior wall of the building and peered cautiously around the frame of the window. Though he could see the entrance to the loft, he was certain that, as long as he remained quite still, his presence would go unnoticed.

Whoever was down there was taking his time, unless he was just a neighborhood bum who had decided to bed down for the night on the first floor. Larsen decided to give him a minute more and then check the window downstairs on his way to the street. The minute wasn't quite up when the intruder showed. He was no local bum.

He was neatly and conservatively tailored, lean and alert, scrubbed face and wholesome looking. He made a quick sweep of the area with his eyes. Then he drew on a pair of rubber surgical gloves just like Larsen's and headed straight for the suitcase. The ingenuous look was just a mask. Behind it there was know-how and deliberateness of purpose. Larsen watched for a moment, amused and somewhat perplexed. This guy was one of the boys; no doubt about it. Larsen wondered whose boy he was.

Larsen slipped away from the window and carefully descended the ladder. Then he ran the short distance back to the corner of Broadway and Canal. He noted, to his satisfaction, that the Plymouth was gone, and Shepard with it. A Chinatown tour bus was just pulling up to the curb near where Tobin had fallen. Larsen hurried into the phone booth in the candy store, dialed the police emergency number, and reported a burglar on the third floor of the loft at the corner of Broome and Mercer. So much for the interloper. He would like to have been able to see his face when the cops came charging into the loft. But he had more pressing business to attend to. He hailed a cab and headed for Hull's office.

As the tourists descended from the Chinatown bus, one of them stooped and picked up something lying near the curb. He studied it for a moment and then turned to the four members of the group who had preceded him off the bus. "Did you drop this?" he asked each one in turn, showing them the picture postcard. None of them claimed it, so he approached the tour guide. "I found this," he said, holding out the card. "It doesn't seem to belong to anyone."

The tour guide shrugged disinterestedly. "Then drop it in the trash."

The tourist nodded and carried the card with him across the street, troubled by the guide's lack of concern. The postcard was, after all, addressed and stamped. On the corner of Mott and Canal there stood a trashcan. He decided to hold on to the card until they passed a mailbox.

Chapter

7

Hull's office was a spare and functional accommodation. The New York branch of the firm kept it available in a corner of its tenth floor suite for the use of visiting firemen.

They had provided Hull with a key to the office, a couple of phone lines, three desks outside in the bullpen for his gray men, and an electric coffee pot without which, he insisted, he would be nonfunctional. Beyond that he was, as far as the members of the New York branch were concerned, invisible. This attitude was in accordance with a long-established company policy concerning those of its members who were operating beyond the boundaries of official franchise. The policy had originally been laid down in the interest of candor, so that only a minimal number of individuals would be obliged to lie under oath in the event of a congressional investigation.

Hull had been sent up from Washington without written orders, but with the verbal authority of the national director, to deal with a piece of business over which the firm had no jurisdiction. Apparently the director, who owed his appointment to the arm-bending virtuosity of a certain influential legislator, was having his own arm bent. A simple matter of making good on an old debt.

Hull was an old-fashioned man, black vested, white shirted, sleeves rolled up neatly over hefty, hairy forearms. Balding, he wore a couple of carefully nurtured strands of hair combed up from the side and across the top of his heavily ridged skull. Craggy faced, nose slightly flattened and drifting to the right, granite jawed and barrel chested, he had the look of an over-the-hill pug.

He sat with his bulk squeezed into a tightly fitting swivel chair behind a glass-topped, chrome-legged table. There were a couple of molded plastic chairs in front of the table, seats unpadded, to discourage visitors from hanging around too long. The electric coffee urn, ceaselessly perking, always full, resided on a small serving cart against the wall. A couple of boxes of Hostess Jelly Donuts were stacked up beside the coffee urn. They never went stale. Hull loved his jelly doughnuts, maybe even more than he loved his coffee and cigarettes. The three items were inextricably attached to his functioning. He needed the coffee to keep him going. He liked to boast that he hadn't enjoyed a full and uninterrupted night's sleep in fifteen years. But he couldn't drink a naked mug of black coffee without munching on a jelly doughnut. And he couldn't finish either the coffee or the doughnut without rewarding himself with a cigarette.

He plucked a paper napkin off a stack at a corner of his desk and with incongruously dainty hands dabbed jelly away from the corner of his mouth.

"Help yourself," he piped in his startlingly flutey voice when Larsen walked into the room.

Hull frowned as Larsen bypassed the coffee urn and chose a jelly doughnut. There was plenty of coffee, but the pastry might run out before morning.

"Tobin ran into a taxi," Larsen said casually, as if that would minimize the dimensions of the disaster and lighten the load of blame, if any, that might fall on his shoulders and Shepard's.

"I heard," Hull piped back.

Larsen bit into the doughnut and used his forefinger to squeegee up the raspberry ooze on his chin.

Hull looked pained, picked up a paper napkin, and waved it at Larsen. Larsen wasn't sure if Hull's displeasure was over the wasted jelly or the sloppy way they'd handled Tobin.

"Where'd you hear?" Larsen asked cautiously, after he'd finished cleaning up his chin.

"Shepard."

"Oh? Good. Yeah, Shepard was going to follow the ambulance to the hospital. How's Tobin doing?"

"He followed the ambulance to the morgue. Tobin's dead." Hull sounded calm enough. But there was a storm warning in the air. His cigarette was burning down, unsmoked, in the big heavy crystal ashtray; his half-eaten jelly doughnut was bleeding unnoticed into the little saucer on his desk. His hands, clenched into fists, were set on either side of his cooling coffee mug.

"We didn't lean on him or anything like that," Larsen

alibied. "We didn't even get a chance to offer him a deal. He just started to run . . . "

"So Shepard told me."

"So, I guess that's the end of it."

Hull came out of his chair so fast that Larsen thought he was going to upend the table. He leaned across it, head down, bull shoulders thrust forward, mad. "The end of it?" His voice sounded like an overheated toy steam whistle. "What the hell do you know about the end of it?"

"He didn't have them," Larsen pleaded defensively. "He didn't have them on him . . . and he didn't have them in the loft."

"Then maybe he wasn't as dumb as we thought he was." Hull dumped the cooled dregs of his coffee into his plastic waste basket, wiped around the lip of the mug with a napkin. He crossed to the coffee urn and thumbed back the tap, sending a sizzling stream of dark liquid squirting into the mug. His mind seemed to be elsewhere for the moment, and Larsen hoped that the hot coffee wouldn't run over and scald his fingers and raise his temper again.

But Hull must have filled that mug so often he could do it in his sleep. He let go of the tap just a hair short of overflow and returned thoughtfully to his desk. "Tell me, Larsen, what would you do if you had a bundle of red-hot material? Would you carry it around in your pocket?"

"Me? I'd find a safe hole for it somewhere."

"Where?"

Just like school. Larsen had hated question-and-answer sessions in school; he had never been sure he'd come up with the one the teacher wanted. "In a safety deposit box?"

"That's the first place we'll look. We'll get a court order in the morning and open up Tobin's bank vault." Larsen wasn't sure whether he had just given Hull an idea or whether he had given a duncelike answer.

"Next."

"Next what?"

"Next place you'd stash it."

Larsen figured maybe he hadn't done so badly. Hull was doing the scenario number with him. "How about some blind drop, a hollowed-out tree—something like that?"

"For Chrissake, Larsen. That kind of thing went out with Alger Hiss. Anyone could find it. If not us, a kid, a stray dog. No. No hollow tree trunk. No hollow pumpkins either."

"I was too young for the Hiss case," he said evasively.

"You can read, can't you? Only dopes leave things in hollow tree trunks."

Larsen looked deflated. "What do *you* think he did with it?"

"I wouldn't hazard a guess. But someone close to him might have an idea."

"He wasn't close to anyone, except Crockett, was he?" Larsen asked.

"What about his family?"

"I didn't know he had a family."

"You didn't need to know. The wife walked out on him long ago, after he got shot up and became Crockett's houseboy. Crockett had him on call twenty-four hours a day. She wanted to swing a little while she still had her looks. She swung pretty good. Left him with the two kids, wound up running with Slats Turley out in Vegas. But you're young; maybe you never heard of him."

"I read about him," Larsen shot back aggressively. "He got

46

in somebody's way finally, didn't he? They totaled him about fifteen years ago."

"And her. She got caught in the crossfire."

"That was Tobin's wife? You'd think the stories would have mentioned that. You know, someone who had been that close to Sewell Crockett."

"That's exactly why it wasn't mentioned. Crockett smothered it. Tobin hung on with the kids for a couple of years. Moved them in with him, upstairs in Crockett's house. But Tobin didn't have any time to spend with the kids—Crockett saw to that. The little girl was okay. She was only about six at the time, and the housekeeper took a shine to her, kind of like a foster mother. The boy was twelve or thirteen, and he was trouble. He was old enough to be bitter. He'd seen too much, heard too much. He held it against his old man and Crockett that his mother had walked out. When he was fourteen, he started getting into trouble with the law, almost deliberately, like he wanted to embarrass Crockett and his old man: vandalism, petty theft, you name it. The more he got caught, the better he seemed to like it. He started making life miserable for the little girl, too. A real undesirable. Crockett had him put in a military school down in Georgia. Discipline, you know. It didn't take. He ran away a couple of times, but they brought him back. Then his mother got killed. He held Crockett and Tobin responsible for that, too. When he was sixteen, he ran away for the last time. Tobin lost track of him."

"He could have traced him. With Crockett's network he could have found him in no time."

"Maybe he didn't want to. Maybe Crockett didn't want him to. Tobin was hard-nosed about duty and responsibility.

Maybe he figured the kid was a lost cause. He let him go. I don't know if they ever saw each other again. But Tobin and the daughter were a different story. Even after she left home, she kept in pretty close touch."

"Do we know where she is?"

"Yes."

"What about the son?"

"He's pretty well vanished."

"We could find him."

"Who needs him?"

Chapter 8

Lance Tobin, also known as Lance Gray, also known as Larry "the Lip" Black and currently known as Lenny Blue, was sitting in a rented Chevy across the road from the Pelican Motel near Biloxi, Mississippi. He had gone through a virtual rainbow of names in the years since he'd shucked off the one he'd been born with, but there had been no pot of gold waiting for him anywhere. He knew by now that there never would be. He'd be a smalltime enforcer for as long as his muscle held out. And then, if he didn't cross anyone the wrong way, maybe they'd let him work as a bouncer out front in some second-rate casino, or give him a chair in the counting house, checking on the checkers who toted up the receipts, within sniffing distance of the heavy green. But that's all he'd ever get, just a whiff. The Turley organization had taken him in because of his mother. But they would never let him near where the real action was, and for that he blamed his father's association with Crockett. At twenty-eight he knew that he was strictly bush league and that he'd never make the majors. Just like his old man, he'd be somebody's gofer all the rest of his life. He was a loser, heir to a family of losers.

The kid in the driver's seat next to him gave him a nudge. He was a rat-faced adolescent with poisonous-looking pimples bursting out all over his face; a kid not much different from what Lenny had been when he'd started out, piss eager and full of hope. The kid nodded toward where a Caddy Eldorado was pulling into the horseshoe-shaped driveway of the motel. The big car stopped in front of one of the pink stucco cottages.

The pair in the Caddy were already pawing each other so fervidly that they were having trouble getting out through the door: a tall, slick stud, a real two-bit Romeo in a pool-table-green blazer and a white turtleneck shirt, and a red-headed woman, who, Lenny knew, didn't have too much going for her, although she looked pretty good from way across the road. From a distance the high-priced clothes camouflaged her forlorn figure, and the thirty-dollar hairdo and makeup job effectively masked her hungry, sagging face. Lenny Blue suspected that she'd fixed the stud up with the blazer and the car.

He opened the glove compartment and took out two right-handed leather gloves. He gave one to the kid next to him and pulled the other one onto his own hand. The gloves weighed about a half-pound each. They were lined with heavy lead foil.

Lenny and the kid watched the red-headed woman and the stud weave their way up the path from the Caddy to the cottage. They were leaning on each other so hard that they couldn't walk straight. The woman was maybe ten years older than the stud and so sexed up you could almost smell it across the road. When they got to the cottage door, he had trouble getting the key in the lock, she was hanging onto his arm so tight.

When they finally made it through the doorway into the room, Lenny and the rat-faced kid got out of the car. Lenny let the kid go a couple of steps ahead. This was the kid's first disciplinary action. They were going to move him up from driver if he worked out okay. Lenny was just there as back-up man, and to grade him on this test.

The kid raised his hand to knock and Lenny grabbed his wrist. "Try the knob. I'll betcha they didn't even lock the door." The kid turned the knob and the door swung open.

The redhead and the stud were pulling their clothes off so fast the place looked like a locker room at half-time. They were so busy with what they were doing and the kid had opened the door so quietly that they didn't even know anyone was there . . . for a couple of seconds.

The woman was way ahead of the stud, and Lenny saw why. The stud had taken the time to hang his new green blazer over the back of a chair. She'd let everything lie where it dropped. She was already down to her skivvies, and she must have felt the draft, because she was the first to look in the direction of the door. The stud was in the middle of pulling the turtleneck shirt up over his head.

The kid was in the doorway, and Lenny was a step to the side and back of him, out of sight. The woman must have thought the kid was a nosey desk clerk from the motel. If she'd seen Lenny, she would have known the score right away, since Lenny had been sent out after her before. As it was, she wasn't scared, she was mad. She quit working at the catch on her brassiere, dropped her hands to her sides, and fixed the kid with a look so mean that he recoiled half a step backwards. "Get the hell out of here," she snarled in a whiskey voice that had a drill-sergeant's punch to it.

The stud popped the turtleneck shirt off his head and looked at her, startled, as if to say, "What the heck did I do wrong?" He automatically began smoothing down his rumpled hair with his hand. Then he looked at where *she* was looking and saw the kid, who had been shoved a step into the room by Lenny. And Lenny was now visible in the doorway.

"Get the hell out of here," the redhead said again. Only this time she *was* saying it to the stud. She was warning him away. She looked scared.

The stud didn't know what it was all about, but he looked plenty scared, too, as he bent over to pull up the trousers that lay accordioned around his ankles. He didn't bother to step into his shoes; he just held the trousers up around his waist with his hands. For a moment he looked hopefully at the open door behind Lenny. He thought maybe he could get out that way. Lenny stepped into the room and shut the door behind him, and the stud started to run for the window at the back of the room, still holding his trousers up around his waist with his hands.

The damned kid wasn't moving, and the stud had the window open and one leg out before Lenny decided he'd better step in. He clamped a hand down over each of the stud's bare shoulders and hauled him back into the room. The stud landed on his back on the floor, and the redhead was coming at Lenny, claws out, yelling, "Leave him alone, you bastard," in that whiskey voice of hers.

Lenny parried her lunge, spun her around, and clamped a hand over her mouth, hard enough to hold her and keep her quiet, but careful not to bruise her. "You should have thought what would happen to him before you started running around. I got orders." The woman bit down hard on his hand and almost lost her teeth on the lead-lined glove.

The stud started to get to his knees.

"Well, kid? Are you or aren't you?" Lenny half turned to where the kid had been standing. The door was open and he heard footsteps sprinting away on the walk.

The stud was struggling into an upright position. "Shit!" Lenny spat. "You want to do a job right, you gotta do it yourself." He landed a kick in the stud's groin. The force of the blow lifted the stud an inch or two, and then he crumpled up in a ball and lay there moaning. The redhead went limp and began to sob, and Lenny's forearm got all wet with dribble and tears. He dumped the woman on the bed and then worked the stud over in a businesslike way with the weighted glove.

The kid had run off with the Chevy, so Lenny used the Caddy to drive the redhead home. It probably didn't belong to the stud anyway.

It was fifty-five miles from Biloxi to New Orleans. She sat in the front seat of the Caddy beside Lenny, all the fight drained out of her, a sad sack of a woman with mascara-smeared cheeks.

"He was such a good-looking guy," she said wistfully.

"He'll get his teeth and nose fixed some day."

"What's the difference? He'll never look at me again."

"That's the idea."

"My husband is a bastard."

"He just thinks a woman's place is in the home."

"He never looks at me when I'm there."

"That don't matter. It's where you belong, or so Mr. Kenyon believes. And as long as that's what he believes, he's going to send someone after you every time you step out of line."

"Why the hell should he care?"

"You're the mother of his children."

He let her out of the Caddy in front of the big, expensive house. "No hard feelings, Mrs. Kenyon. I'm just doing a job."

He waited in the car until he saw the front door open and Mr. Kenyon waiting in the lighted vestibule. She walked right past Kenyon, neither of them so much as exchanging a glance.

Lenny started to turn the car around and was stopped by a shout from the doorway from Mr. Kenyon. He backed the car up to the curb and wondered what was up. Most of the time, if a person contracted for a job, he didn't want to buddy up to the mechanic who did it. Especially on a job like this. Loss of machismo and all. You'd think he'd be ashamed to face the guy he'd had to hire to bring his wife home.

Kenyon ambled down the walk, stuck his head in the window and held out his hand. Lenny wondered if he wanted to shake it.

"I'll take the keys, boy." He had a voice that sounded like a belch.

"To the car?"

"Now you don't think I was about to let you drive off with my Caddy, did you?"

"Your Caddy?" Lenny tried to look innocent. He had thought he just might get to keep the car.

"Kind of community property. The missis dipped into the cookie jar to buy it. You can leave it parked right where it is."

"The kid that was with me ran off with our heap."

"That's your problem. The Caddy belongs to me."

"How'm I gonna get back to my pad?"

"I'll have my housekeeper call you a cab."

Resigned, Lenny handed over the keys, got out of the Caddy, and started to follow Kenyon up the walk. At the door Kenyon turned and barred his way. "You can wait out there on the street. Won't be but a couple of minutes." The son of a bitch didn't think Lenny was good enough to come into the house.

"Fuck you, Mr. Kenyon." Lenny burned and started walking. He heard Kenyon shout something about rudeness, and how he'd ask Jelnick to teach his boys some manners. He heard the door slam. He kept on walking. He felt like turning back and busting up the Caddy. But he kept on walking. His ass would be in a sling as it was if Kenyon told Jelnick. Kenyon was a little wheel in the organization; he just ran a roulette-and-craps joint in Biloxi. But Jelnick's job was to keep the wheels oiled, even the small ones, and to promote good will for the organization. Even if it was a creep like Kenyon who needed a favor done, Jelnick's job was to send a couple of boys to do it. Jelnick liked the jobs done neat and right and with no bad vibes afterward. Well, the whole thing tonight had been a mess, and Jelnick would have Lenny's ass, not only for what he'd said to Kenyon, but for letting the kid run off with a rented car. Lenny was so mad he tried to place-kick a trashcan into the street. It made a lot of noise, but all it got him was a jammed big toe. He limped most of the rest of the way back downtown.

55

He finally found a bus line and got back to his hotel, the Seminole, just a block and a half from the posh Roosevelt and as beat-up as a dowager's wayward sister.

The room keys were in the pigeonhole behind the desk, which meant the kid hadn't come back. There was another set of keys there, too, which turned out to be the keys to the Chevy. Which meant that the kid had more brains than Lenny had given him credit for.

"Your friend said to tell you he parked the car on Hancock Street," the night clerk said as he handed over the keys.

There was a stack of *Times-Picayunes* piled on the desk. The headline on the left-hand column caught Lenny's eye. CROCKETT ON MEND. He bought a paper from the clerk and went into the bar for a drink.

He sipped his beer and glumly read the story about Crockett. He had wanted him to die.

After the lead paragraph, there was a recap of the events surrounding Crockett's hospitalization, beginning with his collapse ten days ago while working in his study. Probably sitting in there crowing over his blackmail files, Lenny thought. He remembered how Crockett used to lock himself down there for half the night and then come up, bellowing for a highball and looking as pleased as if he'd just got laid. Probably got himself so excited that night a week and a half ago that he'd busted a blood vessel. And the old man had found him there; that's what the newspaper story said. He could see the old man standing over Crockett laid out on the floor, and all those hot papers sitting out on the desk for anyone to see. He wondered what the old man had done; he never could decide what to do about anything, the old man.

Lenny finished his beer and signaled for another. He turned to the inside page where the story was continued.

"Crockett Aide Fatally Injured," read the subhead. "A puzzling and ironic sidelight to the news of Crockett's recovery," the UPI dispatch continued. "Michael Tobin, Crockett's lifelong friend and confidant, vanished the day after Crockett was stricken. He was not seen again until last night in New York where, shortly after news of Crockett's improved condition was released, Tobin was involved in a traffic accident and fatally injured."

Lenny read the last sentence again, stunned, and, to his surprise, shaken. But only briefly. In a moment the old bitterness returned. Served the bastard right. He probably was so busy thinking about Crockett that he wasn't watching where he was going. Lenny used to wonder in his most poisonous fantasies if Crockett and the old man hadn't been queer for each other.

He paid for his drinks, left the newspaper on the table, and went up to his room. He sat on the bed, staring at the floor between his feet and wondering why the old man had run off when Crockett got sick. It wasn't like the old man. Unless he was being chased. Unless he'd taken those hot papers of Crockett's. To sell? That wouldn't be like the old man. He'd have taken the papers to protect them, to keep them safe for Crockett. If he'd done that, then the old man, dead, had done more for his son, Lenny, than he'd ever done when he was alive. He'd provided Lenny with a ticket to the major leagues.

Lenny got on the phone and put a call through to Jelnick in Reno. It was two o'clock in the morning, but that was just the middle of Jelnick's day.

"Hi, boss! It's Lenny Blue."

"Oh, yeah! 'The Lip.' I used to think they tagged you with that name on account of your appearance; now I think maybe it's on account of the way you shoot off your face. I just got through talking to Mr. Kenyon. He tells me you got a real foul mouth."

"Oh! That! Yeah . . . well, you know how it is sometimes."

"I know we sent you down there to do a favor for one of our district managers, and you wound up telling him to fuck himself. That's no way to build good will. That's no way to talk to a man whose bride has been balling someone else."

"It won't happen again, Mr. Jelnick."

"You bet your sweet ass."

"Mr. Jelnick, I need the loan of about ten yards."

"You need *what?*"

"A thousand dollars."

"Then say a thousand if you mean a thousand. Why do you got always to talk like a hood?"

"I need to get to New York."

"What for? You going to a funeral?"

Jelnick knew. They knew everything. "Kind of. I need to maybe spend some time there."

"What do you think we are, the civil service? We don't offer paid vacations and retirement benefits."

"It's like the jackpot, Mr. Jelnick. I could maybe even cut the organization in on the action. I could give you first bid in return for the loan."

"*You're* going to do the *organization* a favor? Let me tell you something, kid. Your head is as big as your mouth. You want to go to New York, go. You're off our books."

"Now wait a minute, Mr. Jelnick."

"No! You wait a minute. You're through. You understand that? You got too much lip and too little brains. You're bad news." There was a click at the Reno end of the line.

"And fuck you, too, Mr. Jelnick," Lenny yelled into the dead phone. He slammed the receiver down. Fuck 'em all.

58

The newspaper story said the old man's body was waiting to be claimed by next of kin. He'd claim it, and everything else, too.

He threw his things into his overnight bag and took the creaky elevator down to the lobby. The night clerk was reading one of the unsold newspapers on the desk. He looked up startled when he heard the elevator door bang open and saw Lenny striding toward him, suitcase in hand.

"Is something the matter?"

"I'm checking out."

The clerk was momentarily flustered, then he recovered. "It'll take a minute to make up your bill." The clerk took out a card. "Let's see now. Fourteen ninety-five, plus the long distance call you just put through. That will come to . . . " He licked his lips and started doing arithmetic with a pencil on the side of the card.

"You got change for a hundred?"

The clerk looked nonplused. "Don't you have something smaller?"

Lenny tapped his wallet on the desk. "A hundred's all I got. Otherwise you can mail me the bill."

The clerk had been around long enough to know a deadbeat when he saw one. He coughed nervously. "I think we can handle it. If you'll just wait a moment, I'll have to go into the back." He went into the office, just as Lenny figured he would, and shut the door. Lenny counted to twenty, while he pulled on his weighted glove. Then he went around behind the desk and slipped the lock on the office door. The clerk was kneeling in front of the open safe. His eyes went wide with astonishment and fright. He knew what was going to happen and did the best he could to prevent it.

He slammed the safe door shut, but before he could spin

the dial on the lock, Lenny had pinned his wrist to the floor with his heel. Then he backhanded the clerk across the cheek with the weighted glove. The clerk tipped over sideways, his face split and bleeding along the ridge of the cheekbone. He began crabbing along the floor and wound up cowering in a corner of the room, his arms thrown up over his head.

Lenny didn't bother to go after him. "Just stay like that," Lenny advised, "and you won't get hurt." He began stuffing packets of bills from the safe into his pockets. There weren't many. Once, the clerk made a move as if to scramble along the wall to the door. Lenny took a threatening step toward him, gloved hand raised, and the clerk crawled back into his corner.

"There's only a hundred and fifty dollars here," Lenny complained.

"There's twenty more in the desk outside," the clerk said eagerly.

"Goddamned fleabag." Lenny ripped the phone out of the wall. "Where's your key to the door?" He took a step toward the clerk, who brought his arms down, dug into his pockets, and tossed the key to Lenny before Lenny got too close. Lenny smiled. He figured, scared as the clerk was, he might sit in the corner all night before he ventured out. But Lenny locked the door on him anyway and threw the key across the lobby. He took the twenty dollars and change out of the desk drawer, pocketed his registration card, disabled the switchboard, and left the lobby. He figured he'd have plenty of leeway.

He hurried around the corner to where the kid had left the rented car, and drove away. A hundred and eighty dollars and some change. It was enough for starters. But he'd need some new clothes and walking-around money, and a hundred and eighty wasn't enough. He could pick up some more along the way.

As he drove out across the Pontchartrain Bridge, he remembered his sister living up in the Texas Panhandle somewhere. He hadn't seen her since they were kids, but he'd kept tabs. A guy never knew when a relative might come in handy. He wondered if she had heard about the old man's accident. They had stayed pretty close, those two. If she showed up in New York, it could really screw things up for him.

Chapter 9

They hadn't gotten around to burying their telephone cables in the rural Panhandle, so the tap had been easy. He had spliced into the overhead line in the predawn darkness and clamped on an alligator clip. He had run the tap wire down into his car, affixing the wire to the creosote-soaked pole with black insulating tape so that nothing showed. He had been sitting in the car, parked on the shoulder of the road, ever since. It was now two o'clock in the afternoon.

Wheeler's back ached; his legs were stiff and cramped. His left ear was beginning to pulsate and swell from the earphone that had been clamped over it for the past half hour. He lifted the earphone, wiped the sweat off it with his coat sleeve, and hung it over his right ear. He'd been shifting the earphones periodically throughout the day, and he wondered if, for his trouble, he would wind up with a pair of cauliflower ears instead of just one. Reflexively, he patted his pocket for a cigarette and then, despairingly, let his hand drop. He'd smoked his last cigarette a couple of hours ago. He fished around in the ashtray for a smokeable butt, but it was hopeless. The whole mission had been launched in haste. He'd been in such a damned hurry to lay in the tap before anyone got out of bed that he had neglected to provide himself with anything to drink . . . or eat. And now it didn't seem likely that anyone was going to leave the house all day, although he knew she'd have to get out by around three o'clock. She had a 4:20 plane to catch.

He would know when she left. He could see the house clearly across the wafer-flat plain, although he was parked on a dirt track a quarter of a mile away. He glanced down at the clipboard on the seat beside him and flipped through the notes he had taken, reviewing what he had learned through his vigil.

She had gotten up at 6:40, while he was still working on the tap. He saw the lights go on in what must have been the bedroom. The light patterns began to shift as she moved around the house. She finally settled down for a while in a room at the side of the house which he figured was the kitchen.

When dawn came up the lights went out, one by one, and he lost track of her movements until 8:15, when he saw her leave by the front door and start walking toward her car with something like a briefcase under her arm. She had stopped suddenly just before getting into the car, turned, and run back into the house: her first phone call of the day. A telegram. "Medical examiner's office, New York . . . regrets to inform her . . . her father's passing. Her name among his personal effects . . . to be notified in emergency. Please contact medical examiner . . ."

No visible or audible activity for the next forty minutes, except once, when the front door opened and she took a few steps outside and just stood there, hugging herself, staring straight ahead at nothing. Five minutes of this and she went back into the house.

At 9:15 she placed a call to Southwestern Petroleum, inquiring where she might reach James Means. By now it was apparent she was alone in the house. She was told that James Means would be at a survey site in the Guatemalan interior for the next ten days. She could send mail to the Galveston office and it would be forwarded to Guatemala by air and then into the interior on the company supply helicopter.

Nine twenty-five: she placed a call to New York, to the office of the medical examiner. She said she would be in New York sometime that evening to identify and claim the body.

Nine thirty: a call to the local airport to reserve a seat on a 4:20 flight to Dallas, connecting to a 6:30 flight to New York. She asked if the airline would book a hotel room for her in New York. They would, and would call back to confirm. Ten forty-five: confirmation for the flight and for the Hotel St. Stephen in New York.

At 12:30 she carried out what looked like a bag of garbage and dumped it on a heap for burning about twenty yards behind the house.

At one o'clock she called the offices of Southwestern Petroleum again. She must have been having misgivings. She told them that she did not wish to burden James Means with a problem he could do nothing about, but in case he attempted to contact her for any reason, she wanted the company to know that she would be away from home for a few days. Family business. She would be staying at the hotel St. Stephen in New York. That last call was made about an hour ago, and it was the last sign of any activity in or around the house. She would have to leave soon if she was going to catch her plane.

At 2:55 Wheeler was massaging his lower abdomen with his fingers, trying futilely to break up an expanding bubble of gas, when he saw her come out of the house at last, carrying a suitcase.

She shoved it onto the back seat of the car, got in, and drove away.

Wheeler tore the earphones off, stumbled out of his car, and stomped about on stiff, creaky legs until the blood began circulating again. He did a few deep knee bends, holding on to the door handle for balance, and succeeded in relieving himself of the tormenting bubble of gas, shattering the stillness of the surrounding plain with an olympian fart.

Ravenous with hunger and parched with thirst, he shinnied up the telephone pole and undid the tap. He taped over the incision in the cable, coiled up all his leads, threw them into the car, and drove off in the direction of the house he had been watching all day.

Trusting yokel, she hadn't even bothered to lock the door. He turned the knob and recklessly threw the door open. Then he stopped. The numbing hours of his long vigil had made him careless. He was certain that there was no one else in the house, but he felt he'd better make sure. He had been careless in New York the night before and had been grievously embarrassed. Quietly, he closed the door again. He knocked, loudly. He waited for a respectable interim, and then he went in.

He was in a small rectangular room the width of the house—the living room, from the looks of the furniture. He'd forgotten how small and rickety these rural houses could be. At the opposite end of the living room, a hallway ran straight through to the back, maybe twenty-five feet away. The narrow hallway let onto rooms on the right which he assumed would be the bedroom and the kitchen.

He called out, loudly and cheerfully, just in case: "Anybody home?" Then, confident that he was alone, he hastened across the living room, up the hallway, past the bedroom on the right, a bathroom on the left, finally stopping in the kitchen at the back. He looked neither right nor left, but made straight for the refrigerator, pulled open the door, and grabbed the first piece of solid food in sight, half a roll of liverwurst. He tore off the plastic wrapper and gulped down the meat; the wurst vanished into his mouth like a log going into a sawmill. Next he drank milk, straight from the container. He guzzled half a quart before he stopped to belch. Finally sated, he turned to survey the kitchen. It was neat as a pin. She'd done a thorough housecleaning job sometime during the day.

He looked for a place to dispose of the liverwurst wrapper. The covered trashcan under the sink had been emptied, and a fresh plastic liner had been put in. He decided he'd better just hang onto the liverwurst wrapper and stuffed it into his pocket. He hoped she wouldn't remember that she'd left half a roll of liverwurst in the fridge and a full quart of milk. He thought of watering the milk to bring it up to level, but he decided that would be more noticeable than leaving it half empty. He put the milk back in the refrigerator, moistened his handkerchief with some tap water, and wiped up the little white drops that had splashed onto the floor as he

66

drank. He tried to erase the spots on his necktie, too, but only succeeded in spreading the stain. Then he got down to business and began a search of the house. It took him a little over an hour, taking everything apart and putting it all carefully back together again. He remembered her trip to the garbage heap out back and sifted through that, too; a really disgusting chore, but necessary. He wasn't especially careful about putting all the garbage back in the exact order in which he had found it, but he doubted anyone would notice. When he had finished, he drove into town.

He found a pay phone and placed a call, collect, to New York. *Buzz, glup, buzz, glup buzz, click*—pickup. "United Shaft and Shoring," Margaret chirped. The Texas operator asked her if she would accept a collect call from a Mr. Albert Wheeler in Richardson, Texas.

"Yes, we will," said Margaret in a businesslike manner. Then, when the Texas operator gave them the go-ahead and got off the line, she said sassily, "You'll have to hang on a minute, Wheeler. Mr. Maitland is on the other line." And then, impertinently, "Where are you calling from?"

"A phone booth."

"That's good. I was afraid you might have been in jail again."

"You heard about that, huh?" he asked dejectedly.

"Everybody has. It's the most excitement we've had around here in days."

"I'm glad I'm keeping the crew entertained." He felt very small. In fact, he looked very small. Unconsciously, he had begun to hunch up in the booth into a kind of fetal position. He wondered how long it would take to live down being busted for trespassing in an empty loft. He wondered who had blown the whistle on him. Wheeler, the goat. The news had spread like wildfire through the organization. That was the trouble with the organization. Nobody could keep a secret.

"Mr. Maitland can take your call now," Margaret purred.

There was a hum on the wire as she switched the call, and then there was Maitland's bullfrog croak. "Maitland."

"Hello, sir. It's Wheeler." Wheeler was surprised at the way he sounded. He said his name almost as if it were an apology. Margaret's put-down had really done a job on his self-esteem.

"Where you calling from?"

"I'm not in the pokey, if that's what you're worried about," he said testily.

"That's good. We've just about blown our budget for bail and bribes for this quarter."

Wheeler felt obliged to protest. Once they started typing you as a fuck-up, you were through. "That was just a lousy piece of luck, sir. I think you ought to know that. Some nosey do-gooder, probably. A chance in a million in a neighborhood like that."

"It was no chance in a million, Wheeler. We got a line on who did the number on you. And if we don't start moving our asses on this thing, we're going to finish out of the money. So, tell me, what did you find?"

Wheeler began at the beginning, with his arrival at his vantage point approximately a quarter of a mile from the Tobin girl's house, intending to provide a detail-by-detail account from beginning to end as prescribed in the manual.

"Never mind all that crap!" Maitland interjected. He had no time for Aristotelian refinements. "Just lay it on me if you found anything. You're talking long distance." Maitland gave away his age on that one. Who worried about the price of a phone call anymore? Especially if you've just blown a couple of thousand dollars on bail, bribes, and air fare to Texas.

"Well . . . " Wheeler hesitated. "The house itself was clean."

"Great!" It sounded like an expletive.

"But I did find something."

"Yeah? Where?" Maitland inquired skeptically.

"Out back. In the garbage dump."

"Oh, shit!" Maitland barked.

"No. A letter." There was silence at the New York end of the line. Maitland was waiting. Wheeler decided to take his time. "It was in a bag with a lot of old grapefruit rinds, oatmeal dregs, peas, ketchup, junk like that. She must have been in the kitchen when she tore it up."

"Come on, Wheeler!" Maitland roared impatiently.

"Well, like I said, it was all torn to pieces, and a lot of the writing was all blotted out with grease, but I could put some of it together."

Silence at the other end of the line. Only the sound of Maitland, breathing heavily, expectantly, like an obscene phone freak. Wheeler looked down at the piece of note paper on which he'd transcribed what he had been able to read of the fragmented letter. "Something about 'praying for Mr. Crockett's recovery . . . ' "

Maitland exploded. "You think that's significant, goddammit?"

"There's more. Something about 'taken upon myself' and 'protect certain documents.' Something about asking her to do a very heavy favor."

"Is that what he wrote? A 'heavy favor'? That doesn't sound like Tobin."

" 'Heavy' is my interpretation. All I could make out on the

scrap of paper was . . . 'favor, which I hope you will never have to do.' Doesn't that translate into 'heavy'?"

"Let me do the translating. You just read it, verbatim."

"Okay, if that's what you want, here goes. 'I have . . . documen . . . for safekee . . . ''

"For what? What was that last?" Maitland interjected excitedly.

"Safe-kee . . . '' Wheeler enunciated.

"Safe key! Ah! Now you see the value of reading verbatim. Now, listen, are you sure you didn't find a safe key in the house? Maybe she's got it with her?"

"I doubt it," Wheeler said dryly. "It's not s-a-f-e k-e-y, as in key. It's s-a-f-e-k-e-e—, as maybe in safekeeping, only the last part of the word is missing."

"Why the hell didn't you explain that in the first place?" Maitland barked.

"You said to leave the translating to you, remember?"

"Go on!" Maitland growled.

"' . . . must entrust you with the . . . I have arranged . . . a good and decent girl . . . your brother turned out to be . . . ' You didn't tell me she had a brother."

"Are you asking or reading?"

"I'm asking."

"She's got a brother, we just found out."

"Maybe he knows something."

"If we could find him, we'd look into it."

"' . . . no use crying over spilled milk . . . ' ''

"Who's crying? The brother probably doesn't know anything, anyway. He's been out of touch with the family for years."

"I was reading from the letter."

70

"Oh!"

"' . . . no use crying over spilled milk . . . '" Wheeler repeated and then stopped.

"Yeah?" Maitland asked eagerly.

"That's all."

"That's all?" Maitland sounded stricken.

"That's all I could piece together."

"Where'd you say you found that stuff?"

"In the garbage heap out back."

"How much garbage is there?"

"What's the difference?"

"How much?"

"A pit full, a couple of feet deep and about four feet square. It looks like they burn it out there."

"I want it."

"You want what?"

"I want the garbage."

"What for?"

"You could have missed something."

"You can't just go stealing someone's garbage. They'll notice."

"Wheeler, there are some things so important you can't waste time tending to the little niceties. I want that garbage and I want it on my desk no later than tomorrow morning."

"On your *desk?*"

"You know what I mean. Now, you lure her out of that house on some pretext and get in there with a shovel, and get on a plane with it tonight."

"There must be a hundred pounds of it," Wheeler sighed.

"I want it."

"Okay. At least I won't have to rack my brains for a pretext to lure her out with," he said with a touch of sarcasm. "She's already out. She's on her way to New York. Hotel St. Stephen."

"Why didn't you say so before?"

"We got into the garbage and couldn't seem to get out."

"Okay, Wheeler. Okay. No need to be so touchy. You're doing a good job. There may be a couple of silver bars in it for you if this all works out right."

Fat chance, Wheeler thought. Army Intelligence, Task Force D, had been created and made operational at the special request of very highly placed brass; scuttlebutt had it that the order had come down from no less a figure than General Dahlgren. Whoever it was, if they succeeded in pulling his coals out of the fire, Maitland would be the only one who would get credit.

"You sure you still want all that garbage?" Wheeler asked, in the hope that on reflection Maitland might change his mind.

"You bet your sweet ass I do," Maitland roared.

Wheeler left the booth and went to the brace of phone books on the shelf outside the booth to look up the address of a luggage store. He figured he'd need four footlockers or two steamer trunks.

Chapter 10

Andrea's thoughts were miles away as the DC-10 pivoted on its nose wheel and began lumbering out to the runway at Love Field in Dallas.

"Your seat belt, please," the stewardess reminded her, and then continued up the aisle checking on the other passengers in her section.

Andrea absentmindedly poked around and found the buckle on her left side, but her right hand was getting nowhere in its search for the other half of the strap.

"I think you're sitting on it," a well-modulated voice advised. She turned, nonplused, and found herself staring into a pair of steely gray eyes, set in a strong youthful face. He seemed benevolently amused by her predicament. Patronizing, she decided. But she came to that decision only after she had noted the clerical collar around his neck.

She levered herself up and found the other half of the seat belt. She wondered what he had been doing looking down there, anyway. "Thank you, Father," she said.

He watched her as she buckled and adjusted the seat belt. "That really does make me feel so old," he said. "It's one of the things we have to get used to."

"What?"

"Father. Maybe I'm old enough to be your brother, but . . . " he shrugged.

"Are you a monk or a priest?"

"Neither. At least not what you're thinking."

"Then you ought to have a word with your laundry. They've really sabotaged your shirts."

The man laughed. "Oh! The collar! Well, I'd rather you just called me 'Mister,' if you want to be formal about it. Better still, just call me 'Lloyd.' Lloyd Wade. I'm not a Catholic priest."

"What are you, then, an impostor?"

"An Episcopalian. Missionary."

"You're a missionary?" she asked incredulously.

"Something wrong with being a missionary?"

"From where I stand, yes."

"Where do you stand?"

"I'm an anthropologist."

"I see." He looked chagrined.

The plane began to shudder as the pilot stood on his brakes and revved up the engines. Then he let go and the plane began to roll.

They had leveled out at thirty-two thousand feet and were cruising along on a northeasterly course when the stewardess

74

began handing out the dinner menus. Andrea slipped her menu, unread, into the pouch on the seat in front of her.

"If something's troubling you, perhaps I can help," Lloyd Wade said.

She didn't answer, but edged away from him and stared out the window into space.

"Forgive me," Wade said. "At the seminary they may have leaned a little too hard on the importance of involvement."

She whirled on him angrily. "What makes you think anything's troubling me in the first place?"

"We're trained to spot the symptoms."

"Did it ever occur to you that maybe I'm just scared of airplanes?" She turned away from him again and resumed staring out the window. But she was restless, and after a little while she turned back to Wade again and asked irritably, "What's a missionary doing in Texas, anyway?"

"I came here, not to convert, but for conversion. The training school is here."

"And now you're off to Africa to turn all the pygmies into Episcopalians?"

"No. To New Guinea. But the day of the old Bible-packing soul-savers is past. We really serve as administrators, social workers, call it what you will. If there is an acceptance of our point of view, we consider it a nice dividend. But, mainly, we're there to be of service. I'll have a couple of weeks' special briefing in New York, and then I ship out. I'll have three years in the field to decide if it's all as worthwhile as I think it may be."

"I'm sorry I jumped on you," she said.

"I'm sorry I butted in. Chalk it up to inexperience, overzealousness, and obnoxiousness. Now, at the risk of butting in again, you ought to have a look at the menu. The stewardess is taking orders."

"Maybe I'll have a hamburger," she said without looking at the menu at all.

After the stewardess had removed the trays, Andrea sipped a highball and confessed, "You were right, you know."

"About what?"

"About something being wrong."

She took a long pull on her drink and began chewing thoughtfully on an ice cube. She finished the ice and sighed. "I'm going east to bury my father."

"I'm sorry."

She nodded her acknowledgment. "I've never buried anyone before." The corner of her mouth began to quiver, and she turned her face to the window.

"Maybe I can help," he said warmly.

The sun was setting behind them. The sky had a bright salmon-colored glow. She kept her eyes on the horizon and muttered incredulously but with a trace of relief, "I never thought I'd wind up in the hands of a missionary."

"You were close to your father?" Wade asked sympathetically.

"Yes, considering the circumstances. But there was only one person he was really close to." She screwed up her face bitterly and then asked, as one might ask a sleight-of-hand artist about the tricks that composed his repertoire, "Do you do eulogies?"

"I can, if you'd like."

"You might make that his eulogy; that he had an overdeveloped sense of loyalty . . . to the wrong people. But who would be there to listen?"

"Haven't you any other family?"

"My mother's long gone. I don't know where my brother is, wouldn't know him if I passed him on the street."

"Maybe he knows."

"Why would he come? He and my father haven't spoken in years. He hated my father. He hated me, too. He was one big ball of hate."

"Then he should be pitied. He is a most unfortunate man. Perhaps a little understanding . . . "

"Sure. The Christian way. I suppose he had his reasons."

"Did your father leave any instructions?"

She started to say something, then let it drop. "You mean . . . *that* kind of instructions. I don't know. I'll find out when I claim his things. But I doubt it. He would have counted on Mr. Crockett to take care of everything for him. He was very dependent on Mr. Crockett."

"Mr. Crockett?"

"Sewell Crockett. My father worked for him."

"Ah! Yes. *That* Mr. Crockett. He's quite ill now, isn't he?"

"He wouldn't be here at all if it weren't for my father. A long time ago Mr. Crockett and my father were kind of partners. Not exactly equal partners, I don't suppose, because even then, I understand, Mr. Crockett had that certain quality they call leadership. My father recognized it. It moved him to step in front of a pistol that was aimed at Mr. Crockett. It took him almost two years to recover. Brain damage. Brutal headaches. Mental lapses. He'd taken the bullet in the skull.

"By the time my father had recovered, to whatever degree he finally did recover, Mr. Crockett was on his way up. He was decent enough to make a place for my father. There was a bond between them. But my father was hardly more than the sultan's eunuch. My mother couldn't live with that. She

77

walked out after a while. I guess my brother couldn't accept it either. He wound up doing everything he could to be an embarrassment to both my father and Mr. Crockett."

"And you?"

She shrugged. "I was just a little girl; what did I know then? Some family, huh?"

"Someday, maybe, I'll tell you about mine."

The intercom crackled and the stewardess's voice echoed out over the speaker. "Fasten your seat belts, please, and observe the 'no smoking' regulations. We'll be landing at Newark Airport in approximately ten minutes." The wing dipped as the plane banked into its landing approach. In the distance Andrea and Wade could see the incandescent core of the metropolitan area, fed by rivers of traffic flowing like molten gold.

"It looks like you could get lost down there and never be found again," she said. "Do you know New York?"

"Yes. Do you have a place to stay?"

She nodded affirmatively and then said, "I'd better go to the Medical Examiner's office first."

"I'll go with you, if you'd like."

"I wouldn't mind," she said. "I told you, I don't know where to begin."

"Leave it to me," he said reassuringly.

The plane began to shudder as the pilot dropped his ship down into the soupy urban overcast and lowered his flaps for a landing.

Chapter 11

It was half past two in the morning before Lloyd Wade had a chance to get to a phone and issue what amounted to an urgent plea for help.

"Have you got someone who can brief me on how to conduct an interment?"

"A what?"

"A burial."

The sleepy voice at the other end of the line was suddenly alert and considerably alarmed. "You kill someone?"

"No . . . I . . . "

"Whatever you do, for God's sake, don't bury him."

"I didn't—"

"Take him out to the department of sanitation incinerator on Randall's Island and—"

"I didn't kill anybody," Wade shouted, as he belatedly looked around to make sure no one was within earshot of the phone booth.

"Then who are you burying?" inquired the voice at the other end in measured tones.

"Tobin."

"Tobin's dead."

"I know that. Why else would I be burying him?"

"Why *are* you burying him?"

"Because his daughter asked me to."

There was a long, weary sigh at the other end of the line. "Start all over again, please. From the beginning."

Wade began at the beginning. "You sent me out to the frontier to track down Tobin's daughter, didn't you?"

"I did."

"I found out she was flying to New York. Right?"

"Right."

"And duly reported that fact to you."

"Right again."

"And was ordered by you to get on the plane with her and strike up an acquaintance, if I could. Right?"

"So?"

"So, not knowing the nature of the beast, I couldn't just sit down next to her and offer her my hand in friendship. I might have got it bitten off. I might have spent the next three and a half hours on the plane in the deep freeze."

"Yeah?"

"So, I figured there are two kinds of people a young woman traveling alone might sit and chat with during a long plane trip."

"So?"

"So, I figured she wouldn't freeze out another woman, right?"

"Right."

"But I didn't figure I could pass muster in drag."

"Right."

"So what would you say the other friendly type might be?"

"Oh! Come on! It's half past two in the morning."

"A man of the cloth."

"A priest?" A note of admiration crept into his voice.

"That's what I figured for starters. So I bought myself a collar and a bib. That makes me quickly identifiable as a safe person to talk to. It wasn't until I sat down next to her that it dawned on me, what if she's a Catholic? She might want to talk religion, and I don't know a damned thing about it."

"Tobin wasn't a Catholic."

"Now you tell me. Anyway, I remember something about High Episcopal from when I was a kid . . . and the collar would fit that, too."

"Good thinking."

"Yeah. Well, it was a little sticky at first. I went a little overboard developing my cover. Something else you didn't tell me was that she's an anthropology student."

"What has that got to do with it?"

"I told her I was a missionary."

"What'd you do a thing like that for?"

"I figured it would account for my traveling around. It would make me seem very pure, very good, very harmless . . . "

"Didn't you ever see 'Rain'?"

"What?"

"Never mind, you're too young. The whole damn world's too young."

"Anyway," Wade continued, "it finally worked out. Except now she wants me to handle Tobin's burial. And they never taught us kids that procedure in Sunday school."

"When's the burial?"

"Tomorrow afternoon. Except it may not be a burial exactly. It may be a cremation."

"We can't have a cremation."

"Well, she seems to be leaning that way. Simpler all around. And besides, I didn't know if we could find a grave on such short notice."

"We'll find you a grave. But no cremation. If she's leaning that way, you've got to persuade her otherwise. If she insists on a cremation, we'll have to find you another body to burn. We may want to dig Tobin up one day. You never can tell with these guys. Sometimes they try to take it with them. Did you find out anything about her brother?"

"She hasn't seen him since she was a kid."

"Good. She'll see him tomorrow."

"You found him?"

"No. But there's nothing like a funeral for bringing a family together. I'll send in a ringer. If she knows anything about what Tobin was up to, he should be able to coax it out of her. Where's Tobin now?"

"At The Threshold of Paradise."

"He's where? C'mon, let's don't get carried away with this preacher role."

"That's where he is. It's the name of the funeral parlor. The clerk at the morgue recommended it."

"I wonder what his cut is. Okay. Get some sleep. I'll send a specialist around in the morning to brief you on the burial business."

Chapter
12

It was 4:30 in the morning, and the building seemed deserted. The dolly set up a nerve-rattling clamor as it rolled along the steel-plated floor. The door at the end of the corridor had the word "Inventory" stenciled in black on its face. The two men inside the room heard the cart advancing like a summer storm and opened the door. They were aproned in white and gloved in surgical rubber. They had spread a polyethylene sheet over the table in the center of the room and they were ready, if not exactly eager, for the job at hand.

One of the aproned men opened the lid of the first trunk, recoiled, and turned to his partner. "Okay. Let's lend a hand and get this over with."

The two men reached into the open trunk and began to spread the garbage out on top of the table.

"I don't know why it should smell so bad," Wheeler said. "I used a can of Lysol in each trunk." Wheeler and Maitland were standing in a corner of the room watching as the two aproned men carefully sifted through the lamb chop bones, egg scrapings, apple cores, and other decomposing biodegradables.

One of the aproned men held up a greasy shred of paper, studied it carefully, and then swept it, with the rest of the first tableful of garbage, into a waiting bin.

"Not so damned fast!" Maitland barked agitatedly. "What was that?"

"Scott towel soaked with bacon grease," the man replied laconically.

"You sure?" Maitland asked.

"You want to see for yourself?" the man replied, inviting Maitland to dip into the bin.

"Thank God these people didn't have a compactor," the second aproned man remarked. "Otherwise we'd be prying this stuff apart with a crowbar."

The two men reached into the trunk and began to spread a new and unexamined quantity of garbage on the tabletop. Wheeler's head was buzzing. Except for a catnap on the plane, he had been without sleep for twenty-eight hours. He propped himself against the wall, with his legs out at a forty-five-degree angle. "I hope they've had their tetanus shots." He sounded so thick-tongued that, if he hadn't known better, he would have thought he was drunk.

Maitland glared at Wheeler.

"I'm tired," Wheeler apologized.

"Then don't stand around giving the boys a hard time. Go down in my office and sack out on the couch. Maybe get yourself some breakfast."

"I feel like I've already had my breakfast," said Wheeler, casting a look at the table as he shuffled toward the door. He was halfway down the corridor when he heard Maitland shout excitedly, "What's that?"

"Buttered noodle."

Chapter

13

Across town, in the incongruously cheerful looking glass and concrete structure that served as headquarters for the medical examiner, Lenny Blue leaned over the desk of the night clerk and stared down in frustrated disbelief: "What do you mean he 'checked out' at 12:05 this morning? He was dead."

The clerk, dispassionate as only a civil servant secure in his tenure can be, opened his logbook and referred again to the entry: The remains and personal effects were claimed by Andrea Tobin, who properly identified herself as next of kin.

"But I'm his son!"

"Miss Tobin properly identified herself as his daughter. There was, in fact, among the effects of the decedent a card instructing that she should be notified in the event of an emergency."

"Where can I find her?"

"Her address is listed as post office box 6-23, Hagerston, Texas."

"Oh, for Chrissake! She didn't take the body back to Texas with her at 12:05 in the morning."

"There's no need to shout, Mr. . . . "

Lenny had to think a moment before he came up with the right surname. "Tobin. The name is Tobin, just like my dad's."

"Very well, Mr. Tobin. If you really want to contact Miss Tobin, you might inquire at The Threshold of Paradise."

"The what?"

"It's a funeral home. 917 East Fourteenth Street. The decedent was removed to those premises."

Lenny threw the clerk a disdainful look, turned without a word, and strode away.

"Mr. Tobin," the clerk called. Lenny stopped. "Don't forget your suitcase."

The Threshold of Paradise was a five-story brownstone. The windows of the three upper floors had been bricked over to deprive the inquisitive residents of the apartments across the street of their view of the embalming and lying-in rooms. The stone stoop had been demolished to provide an entrance at ground level. A large black urn adorned with Grecian-gowned figures in bas-relief served as a centerpiece for the large picture window that looked in on the street-level reception hall. In the rear of the hall, in a straight-backed chair tilted against the wall, sat a youthful attendant. He was wearing an oxford gray suit and a striped necktie, but his shoes were off and his head was nodding on his chest.

Lenny pressed the call button and heard a muted chime

sound somewhere inside. The attendant's head snapped up. He looked around blinking, momentarily disoriented. Then he saw Lenny standing behind the glass door. He surreptitiously slipped his feet into his shoes and went to the door. He looked down at the suitcase at Lenny's feet.

"We're not a rooming house," he said.

"I've come about Mr. Tobin."

"Mr. Tobin? Yes. Of course. But Mr. Tobin isn't prepared to receive visitors. He came in quite late, you know."

"I know."

The attendant motioned Lenny into one of the black velour armchairs that flanked the window and the urn. Then he went to a table in the foyer and checked his book. He came back and assumed a solicitous stance. "Yes. The funeral will be this afternoon. But," he added regretfully, "there was no provision made for visitors."

"Look! I'm a friend of the family. I've just come in from out of town." Lenny pointed to his suitcase. "I've got to contact Miss Tobin. That's the old man's daughter . . . " He stood up and reached into his pocket prepared to offer a bribe.

The attendant held up his hand. "One moment, please." He turned and walked back to the book on the table. Lenny fingered the bill in his pocket. The attendant came back. "She's staying at the Hotel St. Stephen. But I'd recommend you don't call for a few hours. She was here until well after one this morning."

Lenny let go of the bill in his pocket. "You say the funeral is this afternoon?"

"Yes, sir."

"Thanks." Lenny turned to go.

"Sir!" Lenny looked at him. "Haven't you forgotten something?" Resignedly, Lenny reached into his pocket again for the bill. "Your suitcase, sir."

At 10:45 that morning, Wheeler shuffled back to the inventory room. The table had been cleared of its garbage and its plastic sheet, and Maitland was sitting there thoughtfully nibbling at a hard-boiled egg.

Maitland greeted him cheerfully. "Hi. You want something to eat?"

"Depends where it came from," Wheeler replied sourly.

"You'll take that garbage more seriously when I tell you what we found."

"I'm dead on my feet. I couldn't sleep on that damned couch of yours."

"One. She was going to get another letter telling her where to find the file. Maybe she's already got it. Maybe she's already picked the file up. I think I know a way we can find out, because . . . two. She's got a brother somewhere whom she hasn't seen since she was a kid. He would be about your age and coloring, if he looked anything like his old man."

"Is that all?"

"It's a damn sight more than we would have had if you'd left the garbage in her backyard. You did okay. Go home and get some shuteye. I'll call you in a couple of hours."

"What for?"

"I may want you to go to a funeral."

Chapter

14

There was a big triangle of land, a hundred acres or so, sprawling in the sooty crotch of two intersecting express-ways, directly under the flightpath to run-way number five of La Guardia Airport. Over the years a number of real estate operators had tried to develop it. Some had gone broke and some had gone deaf, sitting in their portable sales trailers wait-ing for buyers under the acoustic bom-bardment of the incoming jetcraft. But not even the most adept of these sleight-of-hand artists had been able to palm the tract off as desirable suburban property.

It was true, as some of the early adver-tisements had boasted, that some of the lots on the surrounding horseshoe of hills afforded a splendid view of Long Island Sound. But to enjoy that vista the hapless homeowner would have had to pitch his roof directly under one or the other of the expressways whose engineers had been first to take advantage of the high ground.

It wasn't until a visionary fresh out of business college came on the scene that the tract was put to the only use for which it was suitable, aside from being designated a dump. He determined that since the land was unlivable, it should be turned over to the dead, and he made it into a cemetery. He acquired a license and undertook the expense of constructing an impressive iron gate, copied after the entrance to Versailles. He painted and refurnished the forlorn model home which had been abandoned by his predecessors and used it as a custodian's house and sales office. Ready accessibility, combined with a policy of aggressively courting last-minute arrangements, was beginning to pay off. Trianon Memorial Park was an ideal resting place for people in a hurry.

As Tobin's funeral procession, one hearse and one rented Cadillac sedan, drove through the Versailles Gate, Lloyd Wade turned to Andrea. She could see his lips moving, but she couldn't hear a word he was saying. It was as if he had suddenly lost his voice. An L-1011 "Whisperjet" was settling over the car like a giant manta ray, emitting ear-splitting screams and howls as its pilot jockeyed it into its landing approach. Wade shrugged helplessly and pointed out the window to draw Andrea's attention to the polished bronze sign on the gate: "Slumber in Peace, Ye Who Enter Here."

Andrea looked back at Wade, her face contorted with dismay.

Finally the racket faded and Wade said apologetically, "I would have liked to have done better than this for your father. But, considering the short notice . . . " He began raising his voice as another aircraft approached, and finally just spread his hands in surrender.

They turned off the main thoroughfare that divided the cemetery in half and proceeded down a barren driveway called Willow Lane.

"Dismal, isn't it?" Andrea said. Wade nodded uneasily. "But you were right to talk me out of cremation. It leaves no clues." Wade looked at her, puzzled. "Well, we wouldn't know half of what we know about the past, would we, if there were no graves." She gestured toward the bleak necropolis. "But *this*," she said despairingly, "this is almost as bad as leaving no trace at all. Who are these people?" She indicated the headstones, almost uniform in height and color, sticking out of the ground all around them like bleaching bones. "The only story this place will tell is that we were a race that held great store by anonymity." She was growing morose and she knew it. Through the rear window of the hearse in front of her she could see the dark wooden coffin. She continued talking, compulsively, as an alternative to tears. "You know, those old Egyptian kings, with their vaults fitted out like palaces, packed with goods to keep them company. Kids today are told that they were fools to think they could buy immortality that way. But who's to say they were wrong? Here it is three thousand years later and they're still very much with us, thanks to their vanity."

The car stopped.

They got out and followed the coffin on its stainless steel trolley along a macadam footpath. The rows of headstones abruptly ended, and they were confronted by an arid, brick-colored plain divided into half-acre rectangles by a grid of macadam walks. The whole area looked like a table full of black-bordered mourning cards. In the rectangle just ahead of them, two workmen were trimming and squaring off the edges of a freshly dug grave. In the next grid, a diesel-powered shovel snarled and wheezed and chewed up earth with gluttonous zeal.

"They've just opened up this section," Wade said. "They promised it would be planted with grass in a little while."

Andrea nodded disconsolately.

The operator of the diesel must have seen them. He backed the machine off from the hole he was digging and respectfully cut his engine. Suddenly there was almost total silence, except for the distant whoosh of traffic on the highway and the gentle sighing of the wind.

"Would you like me to say a few words?" Wade asked, as he guided her into a position on one side of the grave.

"What for? There's nobody to hear them but me."

"I'll just say a prayer, then."

"If you want to," she said, more out of consideration for his apparent determination to do it right than out of any real desire of her own.

Wade moved around to the head of the grave and took a brand new prayer book out of his coat pocket just as a 707 came howling across the sky.

Hull winced as the decibel level rose until, finally, he let the binoculars drop and hang from his shoulders by their straps while he plugged his ears with his fingers.

He was camped on a rise about five hundred yards east of the gravesite, but the overhang of the expressway offered no protection from the ear-bursting jet scream. To his unaided eye it seemed that Wade and the Tobin girl had their heads bowed in prayer. He took his binoculars in hand again and saw that their heads, indeed, were bowed, but that they also had their fingers stuck in their ears. After the sound had dropped to a tolerable level, Wade opened his book, found a page, and began to read.

Hull muttered an oath. Where the hell was Larsen? He slowly panned right with his glasses, past where the gravediggers and mortuary attendants were standing, smoking. A young man came hurrying into his field of vision. "About time," Hull muttered, and followed him with the glasses as he hurried from the macadam walk over the winter-hard clay and took up a position directly across the grave from the girl. He folded his hands across his abdomen and bowed his head respectfully, trying to keep from panting.

A little smile of satisfaction, almost mischievous, softened Hull's stony features. Then he winced as another jet came whistling down.

Ten seconds later he uncupped his hands from his ears and raised his binoculars again. Wade had resumed reading. The girl appeared to be listening, but her head was no longer bowed, and she looked perplexed. Hull shifted the glasses to locate the source of her mystification . . . and found *two* young men standing across from her, heads bowed. His man, Larsen, had been joined by someone else. Now Hull's expression was as puzzled as the girl's. He swung the glasses to the right and counted heads among the gravediggers and mortuary attendants. Their group was still intact. He panned back to the burial tableau, his mouth drawn down in a frown. Who the hell was the second young man across from the girl?

Hull lowered his glasses and stared grimly out across the expanse of headstones. A metallic glint caught his eye, sunlight reflecting off steel or glass on the rise of ground at the opposite end of the cemetery. He snapped the binoculars up again and panned the far perimeter of the cemetery, searching for the spot.

On the rise half a mile across from him he discovered Maitland perched on a folding stool under an exit ramp from the highway. Maitland had a pair of binoculars, too, and it looked to Hull as if they were trained directly on him.

Hull lowered his glasses, thrust his jaw out in Maitland's direction, and carefully enunciated a string of obscenities which he sincerely hoped Maitland could read, and buttressed them with an unmistakable hand signal, in case he couldn't. Then, in disgust, he focused back on the gravesite . . . and found *three* young men standing across from the girl.

Hull rammed his binoculars into their carrying case and stormed off down the hillside to the place where he had parked his car.

Maitland was in the process of returning Hull's salute and adding a few flourishes of his own when he saw Hull abandon his observation post. Frustrated and fuming, Maitland packed up his gear and scrambled down the slope to his car. He had been so concerned with Hull that he hadn't seen the third young man who had moved into place beside his man, Wheeler.

"Amen!" said Wade, thankfully winding up the funeral service as the whine of another jumbo jet began to rattle his eardrums. He thought that the Berlin airlift must have been like this. He shut his book and looked up, noting the new arrivals with astonishment. He thought, bemusedly, that the way the funeral party had grown, a eulogy might have been in order after all.

All three of the new arrivals looked as if they might have

been cousins: even-featured, youthful, blue-eyed, no distin-
guishing characteristics. None of them would have stood out
in a crowd, except maybe the one in the middle whose eyes
were alarmingly bloodshot and who seemed to be exerting a
special effort to keep them open.

The most recent arrival was the first to move. He detached
himself from the two other mourners, hastily circumnavi-
gated the grave, and held out his arms to Andrea, who,
instead of making a reciprocating gesture, shied backward a
step and studied his features with considerable puzzlement.

Since she seemed reluctant to rush to him, he rushed to
her. Just before he embraced her, it appeared to Wade's
astonished eyes that his lips formed the word "sister." Wade
couldn't be sure, because the 747 that had begun its
approach just as the service had ended was directly overhead
now.

While passively submitting to the man's fraternal embrace,
Andrea twisted her head around and fixed Wade with a
bewildered and questioning look. Ignoring the hovering 747
and Andrea's evasiveness, the young man proceeded to pour
great glouts of words directly into her ear. Finally he released
her from his embrace, took a step back, and held her
admiringly at arm's length. Then he scribbled something on a
card, thrust it into her hand, and turned to go. He stopped as
if he had forgotten something, turned to her again, kissed her
perfunctorily on the cheek and hurried away.

The two remaining mourners, who had stood all the while,
eyes downcast, shuffling in place uneasily while they waited
their turn, now moved simultaneously again. It was the
sleepy-eyed one who finally won the right of way. He
shambled around the grave, stumbled once at the foot, held
out his arms in much the same manner as the first young man

and, in a voice hoarse with emotion or fatigue, exclaimed: "Andrea!"

"Don't tell me . . . !" Andrea muttered, as she again shied backward a step or two.

The young man, mistaking her dismay for a sign of recognition, buoyantly shouted "Yes!" as he closed the gap between them and caught her hands in his.

Larsen, the remaining mourner, who had been the first to arrive, glanced uneasily at Wade while he waited his turn.

Maitland steered his car into the wide roadway that bisected the cemetery, and saw Hull's car about a quarter of a mile ahead, cruising nonchalantly along toward the exit at the Versailles Gate. Maitland jammed his foot down on the gas pedal, burned a little rubber while his wheels fought for traction, and then went roaring down the strip with the zeal of a drag strip racer.

He overtook the startled Hull a hundred yards before they reached the gate, hit his brakes, spun his wheel, and sent his car into a controlled skid so that it came to a stop at a ninety-degree angle to the road, effectively blocking the exit.

He leaped out and strode toward Hull, who had managed to brake his vehicle to a standstill a bare yard short of collision.

Hull's knuckles were white around the steering wheel; his face was turning firecracker red. He flung open his door, hurled himself out of the car and drew himself up directly in front of Maitland. For a moment they stood chest to chest, nose to nose, fists clenched at their sides, pent-up violence crackling like foxfire between them.

Both men exploded simultaneously: "What the hell do you think you're doing?"

Maitland was the first to recover. "I'm trying to find out what the hell you think you're doing."

"What the hell do you mean what the hell am I doing?" Hull piped in his pennywhistle voice. "I'm trying to run an operation here, and you're sitting up there monitoring me. Since when does Army Intelligence mess around in civilian affairs? You're out of your jurisdiction, Maitland!"

"Jurisdiction?" Maitland bellowed. "Look who's crying 'jurisdiction.'" He moved menacingly forward, and the heel of his shoe came down hard on Hull's instep.

Hull winced and sucked breath in noisily through clenched teeth. "You do that again, Maitland, and I'll clean your clock," he said levelly.

"Do what?"

"Step on my toes." He spaced each word out deliberately, trying to control a natural human instinct to lift the throbbing foot off the ground and massage it with his fingers. A ten-car funeral cortege began to ooze like treacle down the exit ramp from the expressway.

"Who's stepping on whose toes?" Maitland demanded, having completely missed the point of Hull's complaint. "Don't think I don't know it was one of your smart-ass boys who got my man put in the pokey."

"I repeat. Since when does Army Intelligence mess around in civilian affairs? You keep sending your bloodhounds out and I'll see to it you wind up explaining to a congressional committee." For emphasis he poked a stubby finger into Maitland's sternum. Then he spun around and took a step toward his car. The arriving funeral cortege had come to a halt just outside the Versailles Gate and was waiting for the entrance to be cleared. Hull stopped, his hand on the door of

98

his car, thought a moment, and then turned again, slowly, to face Maitland.

"Where'd you get the idea it was one of my men who had your boy collared, anyway?"

"I've got eyes, Hull," Maitland boasted. "I've got ears."

"In *my* organization?" Hull exploded, and wound up, again, nose to nose with Maitland.

"*You* figure that one out, Mr. Hull," Maitland said in a superior tone. "And, while we're on the subject of violation of jurisdiction, how do you think you could explain to a congressional committee what your firm is doing poking around in a strictly domestic affair?"

The driver of the hearse in the waiting funeral cortege importunately tapped his horn twice, lightly.

"Why don't you just have your 'eyes' and 'ears' in my outfit find out for you? But you better hurry. Because when I find out who he is, I'm going to hand him back to you in a basket." For emphasis he poked his forefinger into Maitland's sternum again, three times, and turned to go. Maitland took aim with his toe and kicked a shower of pebbles at Hull's departing ankles. Hull whirled.

"Now what the hell was that for?"

"For the finger. If I want a heart massage, I'll call a doctor."

The hearse driver tapped his horn with a little more urgency, and the line of cars in the cortege dinfully echoed his impatience. It began to sound like a traffic jam. The custodian came hurrying out of his converted model home muttering something about disturbing the peace. He wound up futilely waving his arms as the rest of his cavil was swallowed up by the engine scream of an incoming flight. He ran out through the gate to placate the restless funeral party.

Behind Maitland a dark green Mustang nosed out of Willow Lane and pulled into the small parking area adjacent to the caretaker's house.

Hull recognized the driver as the young man who had been the last to arrive at Tobin's grave. The young man got out of his car and peered tentatively around.

"There's one of your boys now," Hull said deprecatingly. "He looks like he's lost."

Maitland turned to see what Hull was talking about, and demurred. "He's not one of *my* men." The young man walked toward the phone booth which abutted the house. He stopped in front of the booth and began searching his pockets.

"Well, he sure as hell isn't *mine*," Hull disclaimed.

They both stared at the young man, who had left the area of the phone booth and was walking toward them. "Would either of you gentlemen have change for a dollar?" the young man inquired.

Hull and Maitland began fishing in their pockets.

"I've only got seventy-five cents," Hull said, holding out a palm full of assorted coins.

"Here's a quarter," Maitland said, dropping his twenty-five-cent piece into Hull's open palm.

."Thanks," said the young man, handing Hull a dollar bill in exchange for the coins. Then he hurried back to the phone booth.

"Now why can't we cooperate on everything just like we did now?" Hull asked Maitland.

"For one thing," Maitland ruefully replied, "it would be against the law."

"Oh, come on, Freddie," said Hull, "since when did you start letting constitutional embroidery stand in the way of

doing a job? We're stepping on each other's toes, Freddie."
Maitland shot him a wary look. "We're duplicating our
efforts. In addition to screwing each other up, we're being
wasteful."

"Waste is the name of the game, Oscar," Maitland said,
entering into the spirit of guarded friendliness. "You know as
well as I do that caseload determines appropriations. If we
start sharing now, one of us is going to wind up short-
changed at budget time. Besides, there are other factors
involved in this operation. Highly sensitive matters, personally involving a very formidable piece of brass. We have to
play it very close to the vest. It's a very special case."

"Well, think about it anyway, Freddie," Hull persisted.
"Maybe we can work something out."

"I'll think about it," Maitland said.

"You know, Freddie," Hull said, saturating the atmosphere
of detente with good will, "I believe you when you say he
isn't your boy."

"And I believe you when you say he isn't yours," Maitland
cooperatively replied.

"Then who do you suppose he is?" Hull asked.

"Do you suppose . . . ?" Maitland speculatively asked as
a sudden thought took shape in his mind.

Hull slowly nodded as the identical thought occurred to
him. And then both of them bit their lips to keep from
divulging any more, just in case the other one hadn't already
come to the same disquieting conclusion: the young man in
the phone booth might be the Tobin girl's *real* brother.

"See you around, Freddie," said Hull casually.

"See you around," said Maitland with matching aplomb.

Waving, meretriciously oozing congeniality, they retreated
toward their separate cars, each intent on getting back to his

101

headquarters and rethinking his moves in the light of this new development.

As Maitland turned the key in his ignition, it occurred to him that he had impulsively tossed a quarter into Hull's hand to make change for the young man, but it was Hull who had wound up with the dollar bill. "So much for cooperation!" Maitland snorted as he rammed his transmission into reverse.

Chapter 15

The young man in the phone booth interrupted his dialing and watched, amused, as the two middle-aged gentlemen leaped into their cars as if in response to the starting gun at Le Mans. The one whose car was parked crosswise to the gate backed up in a gravel-spraying arc and straightened out just as the other car jackrabbited forward. They headed for the exit, neck and neck. For a moment it looked as if they were going to demolish the gate, each other, and the alarmed caretaker who was running toward them, signaling desperately for them to slow down. He became aware of the futility of his gesture just in time to dive for cover as the cars shot through, split-S'ed around the funeral cortege, and zoomed up the ramp to the expressway.

The young man in the phone booth raised his finger to continue dialing and realized that he had forgotten at which stage in the seven-digit sequence he had left off. He depressed the hook, retrieved his dime, redeposited it, and dialed again.

"Special Projects," the switchboard girl chimed.

"Mr. Sturdivant, please." The young man waited. The stalled funeral cortege began to move slowly through the cloud of exhaust smoke settling around the Versailles Gate. A metallic whine signaled the arrival of another jet. He kept the phone pressed to his ear. The funeral cortege proceeded up the cemetery's center road. A single car came past in the opposite direction, heading for the exit. He recognized the driver as the man who had been standing next to him at graveside, the one who seemed to be falling asleep on his feet. When the din of the passing plane had subsided, he realized that the line was dead. He removed the phone from his ear, looked at it as if it had betrayed him, put another dime in the slot, and dialed again.

"We were disconnected," he announced, when he finally got Sturdivant on the line.

"Disconnected?" Sturdivant said. "I hung up. Was that you on the pipe a minute ago, Clark?"

"Yes, sir."

"Then why in hell didn't you say something when I came on?"

"I'm sorry, sir. I didn't know you had come on." Another car passed, heading for the exit, driven by the third young man who had been at the grave.

"It sounded like a bombardment."

"You're not far from wrong," said Clark.

"Did you speak to the girl?"

"I did."

"Well?"

"It wasn't exactly your world's most touching family reunion."

"What do you mean by that?"

"Well, if my sister hadn't seen me in ten or twelve years, I'd expect her to be a little more forthcoming. She wouldn't even tell me where she was staying."

"Oh, Christ! You've blown it."

"I did my best, sir."

"Then what went wrong?"

"How do I know? Maybe she couldn't hear what I was saying because of all the noise from the airplanes. But I went through the whole scenario, just as we rehearsed it. Brotherly embrace. Regrets that it took a tragedy to bring us back together. We're all the family we have now. Bind up the old ties. Everything."

"And what was her response?" Sturdivant asked impatiently.

"She responded by telling me she was very tired."

"That's all?"

"I asked if I could call her tomorrow. She froze me out. The only thing left for me to do was to ask her to call me when she was a little more rested. I gave her my number."

"Not your number here?" Sturdivant exploded.

"I'm afraid you don't have much confidence in me, sir."

"Damn right. Do you know what will happen if this thing gets out in the open?"

"I'm afraid I don't, sir."

"Damn right you don't. Thank your lucky stars you don't. God! I wish I didn't know either."

"I'm sorry if you think I've let you down, sir. I did my very best."

"You want a job done right, you've got to do it yourself," Sturdivant muttered.

"I heard that, sir, and I feel obliged to respectfully remind you that you couldn't have done it yourself. You are neither the right age nor coloration, which is why you sent me."

"If the ship goes down, Clark, I'll personally see to it that there's no room in the lifeboat for you."

"I understand, sir."

"Do you know where the girl is now?"

"Still in the cemetery. Her car hasn't left yet."

"I want you to follow her. I want you to find out where she's staying. Then I want you to call me. Is that clear?"

"That's clear. But something else isn't."

"Yes?"

"Who were the two other fellows at the grave?"

"What fellows?" Sturdivant asked, alarmed.

"I don't know who they are, but they look enough like me to be my brothers."

Chapter 16

Andrea stared straight ahead, at the back of the driver's neck, at the empty hearse in front of them, at nothing. The Cadillac passed through the iron gate and followed the service road toward the entrance ramp to the highway. Andrea's features were compressed into a pout, like those of a child who is obstinately determined not to cry.

They rode in silence most of the way back, except for once, when Andrea sighed and muttered, "So, that's that," and another time when, without turning to look at Wade for fear of breaking down, she said, "I want to thank you for helping. I take back all the bad things I've thought about the missionary trade."

He patted her hand and replied, "It works both ways. I had begun to wonder if we weren't a little superfluous."

By the time they reached the tollbooth

on the Triborough Bridge, with the packing-crate jumble of Manhattan's new skyline just across the river, Wade felt certain that they were being followed. It was the green Mustang that had been parked near the cemetery gate.

When they came off the FDR Drive at Sixty-fifth Street, the Mustang was still behind them. The Mustang's driver had let the space of a city block open up between them and was tagging along down Second Avenue. The Cadillac turned right at Fifty-fifth Street. The Mustang followed at a discreet distance.

As they approached Madison Avenue, Wade asked Andrea if he could buy her a cup of coffee. Andrea nodded yes. He told the driver to let them out in front of the Schrafft's on Madison Avenue just around the corner. The light turned red. Wade cheated a look out the back window. The Mustang was stopped at the corner of Park Avenue, a block behind.

"Do you want me to wait?" the driver asked.

"No, thanks. Take it back to the garage." He handed the driver a five-dollar bill for a tip. The light turned green. The Cadillac glided around the corner into Madison and rolled to a halt in front of the Schrafft's. A cab behind them honked impatiently. The driver started to get out to open the door for them, but Wade waved him off. He hurried Andrea out of the car and through the revolving door of the Schrafft's and hoped the driver wouldn't dawdle. When they got inside, he glanced out the window and saw that the Caddy was gone, and that the Mustang was proceeding up Madison Avenue in cautious pursuit.

"Lloyd," Andrea asked thoughtfully after they had been seated at the table, "you know those three men who came to the cemetery?"

Wade nodded. "I was going to ask you about them."

"They were brothers."

"Whose brothers?"

"Mine."

"I thought you had only one brother."

"I do."

"Do you have any idea why three men would show up at your father's funeral, each claiming to be your brother?"

She shook her head and said nothing, but she looked troubled.

After a moment Wade resumed his gentle probing. "Did they say why they were there?"

"They all said pretty much the same thing. They wanted to renew old family ties." Her mouth curled up wryly at one corner.

"Did you tell them where you were staying?"

"Only one of them asked. I didn't tell him."

"Do you know which of the three is your brother?" he asked cautiously.

She nodded yes.

He hesitated a moment, then finally asked, "Which one?"

"None of them."

"How can you be so sure? You haven't seen him since he was fourteen."

"My brother had a harelip."

Wade looked stunned.

"Did I say something?" Andrea asked.

Wade lowered his head and shook it slowly from side to side, reflecting on the irony of Andrea's casual disclosure.

Andrea said, "Of course, he might have had it erased, mightn't he? The plastic surgeons can correct that kind of thing now."

"Yes," Wade replied. "They can."

Chapter

17

Clark was breathing shallowly and through his mouth, trying to bypass his olfactory nerves. Junkies had used the phone booth he was in as a nighttime urinal; it was permeated with the dizzying ammonia smell of an overused and unattended public toilet.

He pumped two nickels into the slot, dialed Sturdivant's number, and reluctantly placed the receiver against his ear.

"Where is she?" Sturdivant asked without preamble.

"Well," Clark hesitated, "I don't know exactly where she is right now."

"You lost them." There was a note of resignation in his voice, as if it were what he had expected.

"Well . . . yes . . . and no."

"You're not even sure?" Sturdivant asked incredulously.

"Oh, I lost them, all right," Clark said

affirmatively. "But I found out where she's staying. I made a trade with the driver of the rented Caddy. Twenty dollars for the name of the hotel he would have taken her to if she hadn't ducked out prematurely. The St. Stephen."

"Where are you now?"

"Amsterdam and Seventy-fourth, just around the corner from where they stable the rented Caddies."

"The St. Stephen's not far from there, is it?"

"Just about ten blocks. Lincoln Center area. It's like a different world," he added wistfully.

"Then what are you doing screwing around in a phone booth when you could be down there taking inventory of her room?"

"You told me to call you . . . "

"And, Clark, don't bother to put in a supplies voucher for the payoff to the Caddy driver. If you'd been on your toes, it wouldn't have been necessary in the first place."

Chapter

18

He heard the voices outside the door, and he knew it was too late. He snapped the suitcase shut and faced the door, half crouched, like a cornered animal. Were Andrea out there alone, he might have tried to bluff his way through. But there was someone with her, a man, from the sound of the voice. He backed off toward the window, drawing on his weighted glove, and looked out. The outside ledge wasn't wide enough to provide a foothold. There was no fire escape. He heard a key scraping against the lock. Damn! If it hadn't been for the clown who had blundered in on him a little while ago, he would have been long gone. As it was, he had lost so much time getting rid of him and then cleaning up the mess afterward, he hadn't even finished his search of the room.

Andrea fitted her key into the lock

cylinder and turned to Wade. "Thanks for everything, including the coffee and the walk through the park. It all helped. If you ever need a letter of reference, just ask."

Wade reached into his pocket for his wallet and drew out a card stamped with a telephone number and the name of a seminary.

"They give us these in case we get lost. That's where you can reach me if you should need me. How long will you be in town?"

"Another day. Maybe two. There are a few things I have to clear up."

"Remember, then, if you need me . . . I'll be at that number through next week." He held out his hand and she took it. Then he turned and started down the corridor. As he approached the elevator at the far end of the corridor, he heard her door thud shut. He stopped and looked back. She was gone.

The room was neat, clean, and sterile, appointed in that decorator style that is too innocuous to either please or offend: a studied amalgamation of blandness, from the wallpaper to the window drapes. All very depressing. All very loneliness-making. Her shabby tartan suitcase perched on the stand in front of the robin's-egg-blue bed was the only homelike thing in sight. She glanced at the card Wade had handed her and repressed an urge to dial the number and leave a message for him to call her. She dreaded the prospect of dinner alone.

She shrugged off her coat and let it fall onto a chair. The coat was brown and tweedy. More discord for the decorator to cluck about. She dropped down into another chair and stared across the room, past the floor-length velour drapes that bracketed the window like fluted pillars. She could see the glittering plaza of the Lincoln Center complex across the way. She remembered passing a small restaurant near there with a glassed-in terrace, like a Parisian cafe. She thought maybe she would have her dinner there. There seemed to be warmth there.

She decided to shower and change her clothes, to wash away the dust of the cemetery and the scent of graves. She went to the window and flipped the blind shut.

Enfolded in the lining of the heavy drapes, Lenny Blue stood rigid and immobile, his fist curled tight inside the weighted glove. He could see Andrea's hand working the cord of the blind. Perspiration beaded on his upper lip, pooled up in the rill formed by his scar. He licked at it with his tongue. Finally, he heard her moving away.

She walked back to the center of the room and began to undress. She stuffed her bra and pants into a plastic bag she kept in her suitcase for soiled underthings. She looked down at the street clothes she had just dropped on the bed. It would be a good idea to call room service and have them dry-cleaned. She went to the closet and took her robe off a hanger. As she slipped it on and tied the sash, it fleetingly occurred to her that she hadn't left her robe on the hanger but on a peg attached to the door. Maybe the chambermaid had moved it. The chambermaid must have been in the room and done some tidying up and closed the bathroom door, too. Andrea was sure she had left it open, to relieve the boxed-in feeling of the room.

She opened the bathroom door and went inside. Everything neat, neater than she had left it. Fresh towels on the rack, the smoked-glass shower enclosure shut, sealing off the tub. She took off her robe and hung it on the hook on the

114

door. She slid back the smoked-glass panel at the foot of the tub, just far enough to reach in and open the taps. She let the water play over her outstretched palm until the temperature felt right. Then she shut the panel tight again to keep the spray from splashing onto the floor.

When he heard the shower running, Lenny Blue ventured a look around the edge of the drape to see if the bathroom door was shut. Then, moving quickly and silently, he crossed the room, slipped out into the hall, and closed the door quietly behind him.

Andrea tucked her hair under the shower cap provided by the hotel and slid back the glass panel at the head of the tub, and would have stepped right in, except for the fact that the tub was already occupied.

The man was sitting in the bottom of the tub, his back propped against the tiles, his head lolling drunkenly under the cascade of water. Blood, diluted and pinkish, streamed down his right cheek, flushed by the shower spray. Andrea took an involuntary step backward and found herself trapped against the closed bathroom door. Her right hand fumbled for her robe. She tore it from the hook on the door and hugged it to her, as if it could afford protection.

The head rotated listlessly toward her, one eye trying to find her face, the other roving crazily off to the left, as if searching for someone else. For a horrible moment she stood there mesmerized. The swollen, battered face looked vaguely familiar. The man twisted his torso around and flopped his forearms across the side of the tub. His dark suit glistened like a wet sealskin. He opened his mouth, and she gasped. His teeth were broken.

115

She took a step toward him and heard herself asking stupidly, "Are you all right?"

For reply he locked a clammy hand around her calf. Reflexively she tried to pull her leg free, but he hung on tight, his fingers clamped in spasm. Then the hand dropped, smacking wetly against the tile, and he folded up, his torso limply doubled over the side of the tub. If he was breathing at all, his respiration was so shallow it was undetectable. She forced herself to take his wrist and search for a pulse. If there was one, she couldn't feel it for the pounding of her own.

She reached behind her and found the doorknob. She backed out of the bathroom, unable to take her eyes off him until she bumped against the bed. Then she turned and rushed for the phone on the night table.

The line was dead. She stabbed with a finger at the button in the cradle, but there was no responsive click in the receiver. She dropped the phone and ran to the hall door. She opened the door and forced herself to look back into the bathroom. He was still there, doubled over the rim of the tub. She suppressed an overwhelming desire to scream. She pulled the sash of her robe tight around her waist and ran down the hall toward the elevators.

She thumbed the elevator button impatiently. One car, according to the lighted indicators, was on its way down; the other was creeping upward, making interminable stops along the way. The door of the DOWN car opened. As she stepped inside, off the hall carpet onto the elevator's vinyl floor, she realized that she wasn't even wearing slippers. She pushed the lobby button and watched the door slide shut.

A moment later the UP car arrived at Andrea's floor. Wheeler stepped out and looked around, trying to get his bearings.

116

Chapter

19

Some of the lobby loungers watched her furtively, trying to mask their astonished interest in her hasty passage from the elevator to the desk; others simply gaped. The desk clerk, wisely anticipating events far from routine, fled into the office and called for the manager. By the time Andrea reached the desk the manager was on his way out, wearing a professional smile. His expression went slightly askew when he saw her.

Andrea leaned across the desk and stated in a remarkably controlled voice: "There's a man in my tub."

The manager raised an eyebrow superciliously.

"And," Andrea continued, "I think he's dead."

The manager's face collapsed. They had recently spent three-quarters of a million dollars renovating and modernizing the hotel in an effort to attract tourists with an interest in the cultural activities of Lincoln Center. It would do the establishment no good if word-of-mouth—or worse, newspaper publicity—hinted that the St. Stephen catered to eccentric ladies who wandered the halls garbed only in shower robe and cap, or that its bathrooms had become a roosting place for drunks and drifters. "Won't you come into my office . . . please," he hoarsely implored, and lifted the hinged top of the desk to show her the way. "Get hold of Mr. Overmeyer, immediately," he ordered in an urgent aside to the desk clerk.

Inside the office he offered her a chair, which she declined, a cup of coffee, which she declined, and a rationale for what he was certain must have been her hallucination—which she rejected.

"You know," he suggested placatingly, "those smoked-glass stalls refract light in strange ways. Perhaps it was your own reflection you saw . . . "

"It had its hand on my leg."

The manager gulped. "The house detective will be here in a moment."

"He needs an ambulance, not a detective. He's bleeding."

"I thought you said he was dead."

"Maybe he is, maybe he isn't, but a doctor would be in a better position to know than your house detective."

An ambulance, with its attendant clamor, was the last thing the manager wanted. If the woman wasn't hallucinating, and if indeed there was a drunk in her room, Mr. Overmeyer could quietly hustle him out through the service entrance without any of the notoriety that would follow in the wake of a police or ambulance call.

He wondered if this woman took drugs, but he didn't dare

ask, not until Overmeyer had assessed the situation upstairs.

"What's up, chief?" Overmeyer appeared in the doorway, a red-faced, white-haired man with a pitted and rubicund nose and a belly that ballooned over his belt.

"Eighty-six in room . . . " He turned to Andrea. "What's your room, please, miss?"

"603," Andrea replied sullenly.

"Room 603," the manager repeated. "I'll come with you." He turned to Andrea. "I'd like you to wait here, please, miss. We'll have this straightened out in very short order. Feel free to use the coffee urn."

Andrea sat down in the chair beside the manager's desk and crossed her legs defiantly. The manager closed the door and tapped the desk clerk on the shoulder. "I want you to get in there with her . . . talk to her . . . "

"About what?"

"About anything. Show some initiative. Just see that she stays there and that she does nothing rash."

"Like what?" the clerk asked, alarmed.

"Like using the phone to call an ambulance."

"Carpeting looks like it's been dripped on," Overmeyer noted as they approached room 603.

"I don't wonder," said the manager. "She came running down the hall in her bare feet, fresh out of the shower. Do you have your pass key?"

Overmeyer tried the knob. "She left the door unlocked."

"That's why we have vagrants roosting in our rooms," the manager commented sourly, and added, "*if* there's anything to her story at all."

Overmeyer pushed the door open and they went inside. "Room looks undisturbed."

"Um, hm!" the manager grunted imperiously. "That's the bathroom door over there." He judiciously stood back and let Overmeyer open it.

Overmeyer pushed the bathroom door open, looked, and stood aside so that the manager could see. There were a couple of soggy towels on the floor; that was all.

"Open the shower stall," the manager directed, and stepped back again.

Overmeyer avoided the soggy towels, reached in, and slid the glass enclosure back all the way.

"Nothing!" The manager dusted off the palms of his hands as if he had actually touched something. "As I suspected."

"What are you going to do now?" Overmeyer asked.

"Strongly recommend that she seek accommodation elsewhere." The manager started for the door, then turned. "Just one moment." He crossed to the telephone on the night table and lifted the receiver.

"What's that for?" Overmeyer asked.

"She told me the phone was out of order." He placed the receiver against his ear and listened, a look of displeasure clouding his features. He tapped the button on the cradle a few times.

Overmeyer reached down behind the phone and lifted the cable. "It's been pulled out of the wall."

"She did it," the manager said with assurance as he slammed down the receiver.

They went out into the hall, and Overmeyer closed the door behind them. "You think she's a junkie?" Overmeyer asked.

"It occurred to me. How else would you explain behavior like that?"

120

"Maybe she's got drugs in her bags. Maybe we should look?"

"What for? To bring the police into it? No, Overmeyer. If she's carrying contraband, the less we know, the better. I just want her out of this establishment, without any fuss, without any bother, without any publicity." As they passed the linen closet the manager made a mental note to have the room stripped, supplied with fresh linen, and made ready for re-rental that very night.

Inside the hall linen closet the walls were lined with shelves laden with bedsheets, pillowcases, blankets, towels, all embroidered with the crest of the hotel. There was a slop sink, buckets, and swabs. There was a big canvas laundry hamper on casters. Inside the laundry hamper there was a sodden young man, limply folded into a fetal position. And there was Wheeler, leaning over him, his hand clamped across the unfortunate's mouth.

Wheeler listened tensely while the manager and the house detective passed. He waited a minute or two longer, just to be sure, then he let go of the young man's mouth. Clark moaned. Wheeler reached up to one of the shelves and took down a bedsheet. Clark moaned again, pitiably, like someone waking with a dreadful hangover.

Wheeler tore off a strip of the bedsheet a couple of inches wide and tied it carefully across Clark's mouth. "Can you breathe through your nose?" he asked considerately. It occurred to him that he couldn't expect a reply, any more than could a dentist who inflicts conversation on a patient rendered dumb by a mouthful of fingers and drills. Wheeler held his hand under the man's nose and determined that

121

there was adequate movement of air, though not much other movement of any kind. He wondered what they had hit the poor guy with. Then he tore off two more strips of sheeting— apologetically, but necessarily, as insurance against the fellow's reviving at an inappropriate moment and attempting to kick his way out of the hamper. Wheeler bound his ankles together and then tied his wrists to his feet. Thus swathed, Clark was ready to go.

Wheeler wriggled out of his overcoat and jacket and packed them into the hamper around Clark's feet. He took off his necktie and stuffed it into a trouser pocket. He unbuttoned his shirt collar and rolled up his sleeves. Then he took two more bedsheets down from the shelf, shook them out, rumpled them up, and tossed them casually, like soiled linen, into the hamper over Clark's body. He poked around a bit to make sure there was an airway; then he opened the door a crack and checked the corridor. As an afterthought he reached back into a corner of the closet and picked up a mop and a bucket. He felt he'd done everything he could, short of taking out a union card, to pass muster as a porter in case he met anyone in the service elevator.

The service elevator let him out at the back of the hotel in a concrete corridor painted battleship gray, mottled with stains and smelling of mold. He rolled the hamper along the corridor until he came to a door. The door opened onto an inclined alleyway that let out onto Sixty-fifth Street. He paused a moment to think. The man he had fished out of Andrea Tobin's tub was most likely a valuable catch. He had to be transported to Maitland's headquarters where he could be revived and properly interrogated. The hamper was entirely too bulky to put into a cab, and too cumbersome and

122

conspicuous to wheel through the streets of West Side Manhattan for any distance. He would have to call Maitland and order up a van.

He reached into the hamper, fished out his overcoat and jacket, and put them on. Then he hooked the service door open so that he could get back and proceeded up the alley, leaving the hamper just inside the doorway. There was no phone booth on the corner, and he decided that, rather than go hunting up and down Broadway, the most expeditious thing to do would be to use one of the phones in the hotel lobby. He smoothed down his hair, buttoned up his coat, and sauntered around the corner to the hotel entrance.

When he came out again and turned back into Sixty-fifth Street, he saw a Ford panel truck parked at the curb outside the alley to the service entrance, a portable wooden ramp angled down from its open double doors to the curb. That was fast, he thought bemusedly. Then he thought again, and knew it was too damned fast. He'd only just got off the phone with Maitland, and the group's garage was a mile and a half away on Eleventh Avenue. And, alarmingly, a burly man in khaki workclothes was rolling *his* hamper up the little wooden ramp into the truck.

The workman disappeared into the truck with the hamper, and Wheeler broke into a trot. A moment later the workman emerged, and Wheeler braked down to a nonchalant pace.

The workman descended into the alley and Wheeler moved quickly again. He was fifteen yards from the truck now, and he could see the lettering on the side: SANITARY NAPKIN AND LINEN SERVICE. SANITARY was also embroidered on the back of the workman's soiled jacket.

Wheeler came up even with the alley and shot a look

down toward the service door. There were now at least four laundry hampers where he had left one, just inside the doorway. The SANITARY man was jockeying the nearest hamper into position to be rolled up to the truck. His hamper was the only one in there so far. He made a mental note of its position inside the truck. Then he checked the sweep second-hand on his wristwatch and walked on, very slowly. When he heard the rumble of the new hamper on the wooden ramp, he checked his watch again. It had taken the SANITARY man about sixteen seconds to roll the hamper up the alley. Figure twelve seconds for the man to return down the alley for the next hamper. Twelve seconds with his back turned. Twelve seconds for Wheeler to get into the truck and get *his* hamper out. He figured he could make it, just barely, and get clear of the sightlines of the alleyway. Then what? There were no recesses in the back wall of the hotel into which he could duck with his hamper until the truck drove away. But there were parked cars lined up trunk to grill on the other side of the street. He would have time, during the sixteen seconds it would take the SANITARY man to roll a hamper back up the alley, to push *his* hamper into the lee of one of the parked cars across the street. There he could wait until Maitland's van arrived.

The SANITARY man emerged from the truck again and started down the alley. Wheeler checked his watch. It took the SANITARY man a total of forty seconds to make the round trip; that included the time it took for him to maneuver the hamper around in the service entrance. He timed the SANITARY man's round trip once more, with approximately the same results. The next time around he would make his move.

Wheeler started strolling toward the alley while the SANITARY man was still inside the truck. He was almost abreast of the truck when the man came out and crossed in front of him on his way down the alley for the last hamper.

Wheeler began counting in his head, *one thousand, two thousand,* as he bounded into the truck and discovered, to his dismay, that he hadn't quite taken everything into account.

Wheeler's hamper was in the far corner of the van, and there were now three others blocking its way to the open doors. *Four thousand, five thousand.* Wheeler began frantically shifting hampers about. *Ten thousand, eleven thousand.* He had a clear view down the alley. The SANITARY man was reaching out for the last hamper. At last Wheeler had his hamper at the top of the ramp. He guided it with his hand and let gravity take it down. The SANITARY man was rotating the last hamper in the service doorway. His back was still turned.

Wheeler swung his hamper sharply on its casters and shoved it out of the line of the alley. He tipped it down over the curb into the street and started rolling it across, overtaken by a disquieting thought. What if the SANITARY man had shifted the hampers around inside the truck as he had just done? Then all he had was a load of dirty linen.

Fifteen thousand, sixteen thousand. The SANITARY man would be on his way up the alley now with his last load. Wheeler tried to shove the hamper between two parked cars, but the space wasn't wide enough. He cursed, swung the hamper parallel to the line of cars, and trundled it up the roadway looking for a three-foot gap.

Twenty-one thousand, twenty-two thousand. He squinted his eyes against the headlight glare of a car cruising into the block from Central Park West.

Twenty-four thousand, twenty-five thousand. He had visions of himself trundling his hamper down the street like a fugitive coolie, with the SANITARY man in fist-shaking pursuit.

Twenty-six thousand . . . at last! A good yard and a half between a tan Buick and a red VW. He spun the hamper in behind the broad trunk of the Buick, turned his back on the oncoming headlights and reached down inside the hamper to make sure he'd got the right one. He wasn't aware that the car had come to a stop right next to him until he heard the man's voice. "Watcha got there, pal?"

He turned and found himself looking directly at the readily identifiable silhouette of a policeman's cap. The cop had an elbow and forearm draped casually over the sill of his patrol car window and was leaning out inquisitively. His partner was already getting out on the other side.

Wheeler thought of running, but that would have been stupid, if not patently impossible, wedged as he was between the hamper on one side and the police car on the other.

"Where do you think you're going with that?" the cop in the driver's seat asked.

"To the Laundromat?" Wheeler responded lamely.

By this time the second cop had squeezed into the space between the cars along with Wheeler, and had begun poking interestedly around among the sheets.

Thirty-nine thousand, forty thousand. Wheeler held out his hands for the cuffs.

Chapter 20

"Ah!" Maitland grunted into the phone after Wheeler had identified himself. "The invisible man. I sent the truck where you said, but they couldn't find you. Shall we try again? Do you have another rendez-vous point in mind?"

"I don't need the truck anymore," Wheeler said dejectedly.

"Very well, then." Maitland tried to control his temper and wound up sounding as if he were talking to a child. "We'll put the truck to bed. Anything else you need tonight before I turn in?"

"A lawyer."

"A lawyer?" Maitland repeated incredulously, and then, after a ruminative pause: "This has a very familiar ring to it, Wheeler."

"Yes," Wheeler sighed.

"You've been jugged again?"

Wheeler didn't answer.

"That makes twice this week. Once more and you're a three-time loser. Maybe they'll put you away for life. What happened to the guy you said you had in the hamper that you said you needed the truck for? Don't tell me he was a cop and he put the collar on you."

"No, he wasn't a cop," Wheeler said irritably.

"Do you know *who* he was, this guy you say you found in the girl's bathtub? I'm beginning to think he was a figment of your imagination. I'm beginning to think you may be in need of a sabbatical, or maybe even a terminal, leave."

"He's no figment. He was in the tub. He was also standing next to me at the cemetery. And if you want to terminate me, you're welcome to do it. But first do the decent thing and send a guy down to bail me out."

"I'll think about bailing you out. Meanwhile you think . . . and see if you get any ideas who the guy in the tub might be."

"I know who he is. His name's Clark. He's one of Sturdivant's boys."

"You sure?" Maitland was suddenly alert and businesslike. The bantering tone was gone. "Did he have ID?"

"Come on, chief. Who carries ID that's worth a damn?"

"Then how do you know?"

"He was coming around in the police car on the way to the hospital. They took him to the hospital before they took me to the jug. He was still punchy and they asked him who he was and he said, kind of proudlike, or as proud as he could manage, being only half conscious, 'Clark, DSA. Call Mr. Sturdivant.' Then he looked at me like he was fixing my face in his memory. He only had one good eye, but there was murder in it. And then he passed out again."

"What have they got you booked for?"

"Aggravated assault for sure. They're thinking about throwing in a little kidnapping charge, too."

"Okay, Wheeler. I'll have you out first thing in the morning."

"The morning?!" Wheeler protested. "Why not now?"

"Second midnight call in a week, Wheeler. I've got to let our miracle-working attorney get some sleep or he's liable to refund his retainer and walk out on us."

Chapter

21

Maitland dropped the receiver back into its cradle, pivoted his chair around, and planted his feet up on the windowsill. He lit a cigarette and leaned back in the chair. He sighted through the "V" formed by the angle of his shoes and mentally began shooting out the lights in the buildings across the river in New Jersey. He was a belly gunner again on a B-29, long ago, when life was simpler and issues were sharply defined.

This business with Sturdivant's man was unsettling. He had known about Hull's efforts to outmaneuver him almost from the start. Sturdivant represented a disturbing new element. Sturdivant was a special projects administrator in the Domestic Security Agency, which was Crockett's own organization. He wondered if Sturdivant had just come in, or if he'd been there all along, operating in the shadows.

The latter possibility opened the door to speculation that other groups might also be operating in this area, including agencies from the other nine-tenths of the world, allegedly friendly or openly unfriendly, whom he grouped together under that great dark umbrella he called "the other side."

He was entertaining visions of a clandestine Armageddon and pumping imaginary tracer bullets into an oil barge on the river when the phone rang. He let the oil barge go and picked up the receiver.

It was Sturdivant, his voice crackling with outrage. "If it's war you want, you'll have it, Maitland."

Maitland replied to the challenge with aplomb. "Give me a point of reference and maybe I'll know what we're supposed to be fighting about."

"Assault, Maitland. And abduction. That kind of thing may be okay when you're operating overseas, but it doesn't go here. There are constitutional safeguards, you know."

"What makes you think it was my man who hit your man?" Maitland inquired dispassionately.

"I have my sources. And I know you. Who else would be messing around in an affair that's none of his business anyway?"

"Hull," Maitland suggested.

There was a long silence at the other end while Sturdivant digested this chunk of gristle. When he came back, he sounded chastened, almost contrite. "Hull?"

"Hull."

"Was it Hull's man who zapped my man?" He managed to get a little belligerence back into his tone.

"I honestly don't know."

Sturdivant considered this a moment and then said portentously, "Maitland, I think we may be on a collision course—the three of us."

"I think you may be right," Maitland agreed.

"I think we all ought to sit down together and get our signals straight or somebody's going to get killed."

"I think that's something worth talking about."

"First thing tomorrow, if Hull is available?"

"Any time."

"My office?"

"Oh, come on, Sturdivant. You know better than that."

"Well, certainly not your office," Sturdivant shot back.

"Certainly not, much as I'd like to."

"Nor Hull's."

"Nor Hull's."

"Neutral ground?"

"Neutral ground."

"I'll find a location, contact Hull, and get back to you."

"Remember. What's neutral to you may not be neutral to me."

"Trust me," Sturdivant said with remarkable assurance considering the circumstances, and hung up.

Chapter 22

Well, maybe she didn't look as if she'd just stepped out of Neiman-Marcus, or whatever the New York equivalent was, but she didn't look really raunchy either. Nevertheless, Andrea had the uneasy feeling that she was under observation. She'd sensed it ever since she'd come down for breakfast. Residual paranoia after last night's unpleasantness, maybe. The other people in the coffee shop seemed innocent enough, slightly puffy eyed, sleepily stoking up. There were a young man and woman about her age, sharing secrets and tasting from each other's plates. Honeymooners? There was an aging matron with blue-rinsed hair, nibbling at buttered toast and sipping coffee. A couple of blustery conventioneers trying out their latest jokes on their long-suffering waitress seemed harmless, if somewhat obnoxious. The window in front looked out onto the park. There were lines of waiting cabs on Central Park South, but no one out there seemed interested in what was going on inside. Behind her was an interior window that gave onto the hotel lobby. Except for the occasional passerby who stopped to check the menu affixed to the lobby window, there was no one there who seemed especially interested in the coffee shop. Still, she couldn't shake the feeling that someone was looking over her shoulder.

"Everything all right, ma'am?" the waitress asked.

"Delicious."

"Freshen up your coffee?"

"Thank you."

The waitress filled her cup from a steaming beaker.

"And I'll have the check, please."

The waitress nodded and went away.

The pancakes had been dollar-sized, wafer thin and delicious. She cut the last one into quarters, stacked the quarters up with her fork, speared them, and sponged up the residue of syrup. She glanced at her wristwatch. 9:40. That would make it 8:40 Texas time, and Charlie Flemming would be opening up the post office in Hagerston. Her father's last letter to her had indicated that she might expect another communication. She decided she'd call Charlie Flemming and ask him to check her box.

She paid her bill and discovered that the coffee shop's famous dollar-sized pancakes lived up to their name. They'd cost just about a dollar apiece. And they'd charged her for the second cup of coffee, too.

She went back to her room and put the call through to Charlie Flemming.

"Howdy, Miz Tobin. I thought you'd gone east."

"I'm in New York now."

"Something about daddy, I heard. I'm truly sorry about that, ma'am."

"Thank you, Charlie. Can I ask a favor?"

"Anything you say, Miz Tobin."

"Would you take a look at my box? I was expecting a letter."

"Just a minute, Miz Tobin." He was back in less than a minute. "Sorry to keep you waiting. Now let's see what we have here. Couple of pieces of junk mail. You don't care about them, do you?"

"What else?"

"Magazine. *Scientific American.* Something from the bank, it looks like."

"The local bank?"

"That's right."

"What else?"

"Picture postcard . . . and a letter."

"Where's the letter from, Charlie?"

"Well, it's postmarked with some Mexican-looking name. No, not Mexican neither. I see by the stamp, now, it's Guatemala. James Means, it says on the back flap. That's your feller, ain't it?" Charlie asked significantly. Although Andrea and Jim had borne the expense of maintaining separate mailboxes, Charlie Flemming suspected a relationship and took a prurient interest in its progress.

"Is the postcard from there, too?" she asked.

"The postcard? Why, no." A pause while he turned it over. His voice took on a solemn tone. "It's from your daddy."

"Will you read what it says, please, Charlie?"

"Well, it don't say nothing, Miz Tobin." He sounded apologetic. "He just signed it in the place where the message should be. It just says, 'Love, Dad.' "

"Where did it come from, Charlie?"

"Well, that's mighty strange," he said ruminatively.

"What, Charlie?"

"The postmark is New York. But the card. It's a picture postcard, like I told you, and the card is of a place called Barrows Island."

"And there's no message on it?"

"Just the picture on the one side and the signature on the other. And your name and address, of course. Was he staying on this Barrows Island when he passed?"

"No, Charlie . . ."

". . . because he's marked a little X on the picture."

"What do you mean, Charlie?"

"Well . . . you know, the way people will mark an X where their room is in a hotel or the like."

"Charlie," she asked eagerly, "what's the picture of?"

"Well, it's mostly like a beach. You know, as it would be viewed coming in from the sea. A very pretty beach, sand and boulders, and a cliff rising behind. Looks like the white cliffs of Dover."

"And he marked the X on the beach?" she asked incredulously.

"Oh! No, ma'am. Not on the beach, exactly. Up on top of them cliffs, there's what looks like a few houses spotted here and there. That's where he made the mark, top of them cliffs. That's why I figured maybe he was stopping there when he passed."

Andrea squeezed her eyes shut and tried to visualize the scene. The approach from the sea. The beach. The cliffs, the houses. But Barrows Island, as she recalled it, was walled by cliffs on three sides. It was a tiny island. Roughly two miles long and maybe a mile and a half wide at its widest place.

Shaped like a lobster claw, with a bay at the opening. From Charlie's description, the picture might have been taken from any one of three sides of the island. "Charlie," she asked, trying to keep her voice under control, "if you put that postcard into an envelope and sent it to me here in New York, how long would it take to arrive?"

"Airmail?"

"The very fastest way."

"That'd be airmail, special delivery."

"How long?"

"Well, special delivery, I'd have the boy take it right out to the airport. There's a . . . hold on a minute now . . . you bet . . . he could have it on the 9:30 plane connecting with Dallas. With a little luck and hitting all the connections right, you might have it in your hands by evening."

"Would you do that for me, Charlie? I'll pay for the postage when I get back there."

"My pleasure, Miz Tobin."

"Thank you, Charlie."

She gave him her address at the hotel.

Then she put on her coat and hurried downstairs.

Chapter

23

In the middle of Central Park there is a lake. You can row a rented boat on it in the summer, or ice skate on it in the winter. People occasionally fish in it, though how the fish get there is a mystery, since the lake was manmade. Every now and then a kid will sneak a swim in it, though swimming there is against the law and decidedly unsalubrious.

There's a boathouse fronting on the lake. In the summer you can rent your boats there; in the winter you can rent ice skates. They sell snacks and sandwiches in the boathouse, too, and there are tables on the flagstone terrace, open to waterborne breezes in the summer, enclosed in glass and heated in the winter, with a fine sylvan view in any season.

Fifty yards up a footpath from the boathouse there is a modest-sized parking field with room for thirty or forty cars.

There was a sprinkling of skaters on the lake at nine o'clock that morning. A couple of people were having coffee and doughnuts on the boathouse terrace, but there were, as yet, no cars in the parking lot when Maitland drove in. He was the first to arrive, and, as agreed, he was alone: no chauffeur, no secretary, no sidemen. He turned off his engine, glanced around, tapped lightly with a fingernail against the middle button of his overcoat and confidentially intoned: "Testing, testing. This is Mother Eagle. Do you read me, chicks?"

He flipped on the car radio, pressed the button for a preset short-wave frequency, and listened.

"Chickens here. We read you, Mother. Five by five."

"Roger, chicks. Test is ended. No more transmissions from your side. Keep your feathers dry and your tape running. My mike is open. Here they come." He turned the receiver off on his car radio and watched as Sturdivant's car rolled into a space a few yards away. Sturdivant was alone, in accordance with the ground rules, as was Hull, who followed Sturdivant in. Hull parked about twenty yards downfield from Sturdivant and Maitland, so that their cars were positioned like the three points of a triangle. The three men got out and converged on a spot at the approximate center of the triangle. Handshakes all around. Lots of bonhomie, mixed with guarded glances right and left to make sure that no one had sidemen salted away in the shrubbery.

"Well!" Sturdivant declared heartily, after the greetings had been dispensed with. "Suppose we all sit down in my car and get down to business."

"Why *yours?*" Maitland asked contentiously.

"I'm the one who called the meeting."

"Not on your life," Hull chirped in his flutey voice. "The

ground rules called for neutral territory. If your car's like my car, it's a broadcasting booth on wheels."

Sturdivant looked aggrieved. "Suit yourself."

"How about the boathouse terrace?" Hull suggested.

"Nix on that," Maitland shot back.

"What's wrong with it?"

"You suggested it, that's what's wrong with it. You must have a reason."

Hull spread his hands innocently. "Best reason in the world. They've got coffee and jelly doughnuts there. We can make ourselves comfortable."

"You may be comfortable. Not me. I don't have a man in there sitting at one of the tables with a tape deck in his lap."

"You saying I have?" Hull asked fractiously.

"I think this is a hell of a way to begin a conciliatory meeting," Sturdivant complained. "I think if we're to get anywhere we've got to start trusting each other a little."

"All right," Hull piped, "suppose we start by unloading our hardware."

"Do you think I'd come here carrying a piece?" Sturdivant protested.

"You know what I think you're carrying. Let me prove myself wrong."

"You want to search me?" Sturdivant looked aggrieved.

"I want to search both of you," Hull corrected him.

"That's hardly practical out here," Sturdivant demurred. "Suppose a cop walked by. It would look like a mugging."

"I think Sturdivant's right," Maitland said. "Are we gentlemen, or aren't we?"

"Let's find out," Hull said. "There's a john in the boathouse."

Sturdivant and Maitland shrugged and reluctantly followed

140

Hull down the path. When they got to the boathouse, Sturdivant held the door, let his colleagues pass through first, and nonchalantly disposed of his pack of Marlboro's while their backs were turned. Unfortunately, the wire basket beside the entrance was empty and the cigarette pack struck the sheet metal bottom with a clang. Maitland and Hull stopped and turned. Maitland reached down into the wastebasket and picked up Sturdivant's Marlboro pack. He hefted it in his palm.

"Heavy smoker, are you, Sturdivant?" he asked insinuatingly and passed the leaden cigarette pack to Hull. Hull flipped up the top and exposed the compact tape recorder inside.

"What was that supposed to be for?" Maitland asked Sturdivant.

"Minutes of the meeting," Sturdivant lamely replied. "You'd each have got a transcript."

"NT-66," Hull nodded approvingly. "Pickup range fifteen feet, speed ¼ IPS, thirty minutes' duration. Latest equipment. Very neat. I've ordered some myself." He removed the tiny cassette, tossed it into the wastebasket, and handed the empty machine back to Sturdivant. "Is that a blush of shame," he asked, "or is it just Jack Frost nipping at your cheeks?"

"Let's get on with it," Sturdivant snapped testily. "I've got a man in the hospital with his brains maybe scrambled."

They went into the men's room, which was spick and span and smelled strongly of disinfectant from the morning cleaning. No puddles around the urinals yet, no unflushed toilets, and yesterday's graffiti freshly effaced from the tiled walls.

141

"Okay," Hull said. "I'll do you, Maitland. You do Sturdi-vant, and Sturdivant can do me. Off with the coats."

Maitland was in trouble, right away. He couldn't get his coat all the way open. The thread-thin aerial wire that ran from the microphone in his coat button up his sleeve and down to his cufflink had become fouled in his necktie. Hull located the source of Maitland's trouble, sawed the button off with his pocket knife, and flushed it down the toilet.

"I hope your monitor won't think you've drowned," he said.

Sturdivant looked distressed. His NT-66 recorder had been neutralized, its reel of tape lying in the trashcan outside. He had nothing more to hide. But he didn't know to what extremes of deception Maitland and Hull might have gone. "I think," he announced, "that we'd better go about this most thoroughly if we're to carry on our meeting in any way approximating a spirit of good will."

They had been going about it most thoroughly for about five minutes, picking over every article of one another's clothing like monkeys hunting for fleas. Sturdivant was in his undershorts, Hull was down to his socks, and Maitland was wearing nothing at all, except his shoes, which had already been examined. The rest of their clothing dangled from hooks on the wall like sides of salted cod hanging out to dry.

The door burst open and a young man strode into the washroom. He carried an overnight bag in one hand and a pair of ice skates slung over his shoulder, and the cold was coming off him in waves. The three men stopped what they were doing and stared at him in dismay. The young man took in the scene with surprising composure, waved a hand in greeting, and announced, "Man! It's great out there today."

142

Then he opened his overnight bag, unpacked and hung a neat blue business suit on the only free hook, and proceeded to change out of the jeans and skating sweater he was wearing. "Going or coming?" he asked brightly.

"Just . . . going . . . " Hull muttered as he hastily redressed himself.

"Better hurry, then, before the crowds start arriving. No better way to start the day . . . except maybe a jog around the reservoir."

The three men hastily finished throwing on their clothes. "See you around," the skater called as Hull, Sturdivant, and Maitland made for the door. No additional bugs had been found on either Maitland or Sturdivant. But the search of Hull had produced the most perplexing results of all. He was absolutely clean.

As they stood near the steam tables in the boathouse, Hull asked, with the arrogance of the righteous, "Would you gentlemen be ready to meet over coffee and doughnuts now?"

"No."

Hull spread his hands. "Then I don't know what else to suggest, except maybe take that young man's advice and get out onto the lake before the crowds arrive."

"That's not a bad idea at all," said Maitland.

"Agreed," said Sturdivant. "We'll walk out about a hundred yards, to the middle of the cove. I think that should be safe."

They clumped down the long wooden ramp to the lakeside, where a shivering Parks Department employee blocked their way. "Nobody goes on the lake without skates," he said.

"But we don't have skates," Sturdivant explained.

"Then you don't go on the lake."

"Do you rent skates?" Hull asked.

"In the boathouse."

"Of course," Sturdivant said. "That's why they won't let anybody on the lake without skates."

They rented their skates in the boathouse, left their shoes behind as security, clumped back down the ramp on wobbly ankles, and slipped, slithered, and windmilled their way into the middle of the cove. The Parks Department man, watching them, shook his head in bewilderment and muttered, "Health nuts!"

They achieved a precarious stability in the middle of the cove by forming a circle and holding onto one another's shoulders for support. They might have been a trio of drunks about to launch into a chorus of "Sweet Adeline."

"Okay, Sturdivant," Hull piped. "You called the meeting. You've got the chair."

"I'd rather have the floor if you don't mind. There are some things I want to say."

"For p-pete's sake," Maitland stammered through chattering teeth, "c-can't we f-forget R-Robert's Rules of Order? I'm f-freezing my ass off."

"All right," Sturdivant said. "Then let's start out by leveling with each other. Fact. Crockett's in the hospital. Fact. He may come out of it with all his marbles intact. He may come out a vegetable. He may even have a relapse and not come out at all. We can hope for one of the two latter alternatives, but we can't count on them. But while he's invalided, he's vulnerable. Now, we're all aware that he maintained certain extremely delicate files . . . " He looked at Hull and Maitland

144

for confirmation. Hull shrugged, noncommittally; Maitland merely shivered.

"Okay," Sturdivant snapped testily. "I'll tell you then, for a fact. He has something on everyone who counts or who might count one day, from a couple of promising Senate page boys, right through to both political parties' most likely candidates for the national ticket in the next election. He knows where all the bodies are buried and in whose closets all the skeletons are hiding. He's got everything covered, from sodomy to sedition. He can sink the whole damn ship if he chooses to pull the plug."

"So, what are you proposing?"

"Cooperation. Let's quit acting at cross-purposes. Let's pool our efforts and our finds."

"Th-that's re-really generous of you. Especially s-since there's no f-file on your b-boss."

"Oh? Isn't there?" Sturdivant asked.

"Crockett kept a file on his own first deputy?" Hull piped incredulously.

"How do you think he kept control? Charisma? You have my word, if we work together, each organization gets its own file to burn or shred or flush down the toilet, or preserve for posterity, if you want to. Then, even if Crockett comes out of that hospital with all his marbles, we'll have pulled his teeth. There'll be nothing for him to do but head out to pasture."

"Wh-who g-gets the other f-files?"

"What other files?" Sturdivant asked ingenuously.

"The ones on everybody from promising page boys to presidents."

"What's that got to do with it?"

"P-plenty. Whoever g-gets the b-bulk of Crockett's files has Crockett's muscle."

"I really hadn't thought about it," Sturdivant mendaciously replied.

"The hell you hadn't," Hull piped angrily.

"The organization that g-gets h-hold of those f-files becomes numero uno."

"Never mind organizations. What about individuals?" Hull asked, with an accusing look directed at Sturdivant. "Any individual who gets hold of those files can write his own ticket. If he wants power, he's got it. If he wants money, he's an instant millionaire."

"Hmmm," said Sturdivant thoughtfully. "I'm willing to consider that." Hull and Maitland stared at him in astonishment. "Just the three of us," Sturdivant suggested. "Think about it."

"I am," said Hull. "And I'm wondering which one of us would be left standing after the long knives had been packed away."

"Nonsense," said Sturdivant reassuringly. "There'd be plenty to go around."

"Would there be?" Hull asked skeptically.

"You have my word." He raised his arm as if to take an oath on it and lost his balance. Hull and Maitland jeopardized their own shaky equilibrium in a reflex effort to hold him upright. Their feet shot out from under them and they sat down, hard, on the ice. Sturdivant, to his chagrin, was the only one of the three who remained standing.

Chapter 24

Lloyd Wade's nose was numb and his ears ached with the cold. He was standing at the side of the Seventy-second Street transverse, stamping his feet to keep them alive and beating at his chest with his mittened hands, when he saw the lone car coming around the curve from the direction of the boathouse. He raised his thumb hitchhiker style and tried to effect a smile, but his mouth wasn't moving very well, and the result was something like a grimace, which in fact reflected his state of mind.

Hull checked his mirror to make sure there was no one behind him and brought his car to a stop. Wade pulled open the door and plopped down inside.

"Thanks a lot," he exhaled, clouding up the window in front of him. "What took you so long? You got off the lake twenty minutes ago."

Hull started the car rolling toward Central Park West. "After all the business talk was over, Sturdivant insisted on buying a round of coffee and doughnuts inside the boathouse. You know, spirit of detente. Did you get everything?"

"About two-thirds of it. Almost all of Sturdivant and most of Maitland. You had your back to us."

"Of course. Where's the lip reader now?"

"Back at the office transcribing from the shorthand. He was really turning blue. I practically had to pry the binoculars off his eyelids when he was finished. Funny thing, though."

"Yeah? What?" Hull turned left where the road branched just before the exit at Central Park West, and headed downtown on the north-south transverse.

"I didn't know Maitland had a speech defect."

"A speech defect?"

"The lip reader said he was stuttering."

Hull smiled. "Yeah!"

"Are you really going to cooperate?"

"Am I a man of my word?" He glanced at Wade, who didn't reply. "For my part, I promised them I'd pull Larsen out."

"Why?"

"Why not? There were three guys out in that graveyard claiming to be her brother: Larsen; a guy named Wheeler, who belongs to Maitland; and a guy named Clark, who belongs to Sturdivant and who has been slightly maimed. I agreed to let Wheeler carry the ball for the three of us."

"Can you trust Maitland that far?"

"What's the difference? You told me that the Tobin girl knows that none of the three guys out there was her brother."

"What about me?"

"I gave my word on Larsen. Nobody knows about you. Where is she now?"

"She changed hotels."

"I don't blame her."

"She's at The Brittany, on Central Park South."

"Why do you figure she's hanging around?"

"What makes you think she's hanging around? She buried the old man yesterday. She had to sleep somewhere last night. Maybe she's going home today. I don't call that hanging around."

"I don't call that kind of thinking professional," Hull piped reprimandingly. "Always presume guilt until proof of innocence is established. I think she's hanging around." He turned on the car's two-way radio and put in a call to his office. "Who's tagging the Tobin girl?"

"From whose department?"

"What do you mean, whose department?"

"She's got more ticks on her than a stray cat."

"Cooperation!"

"Say again?"

"Never mind. Whose on her from *our* department?"

"Shepard."

"What's the sheet on her?"

There was a pause while they pulled the sheet. "8:15, breakfast in the hotel coffee shop. 8:45, back to her room. 9:15, down in the lobby again; she's got an overcoat on. She stops at the desk. Looks like the clerk is giving her directions somewhere. He gives her a street map and marks it for her. 9:20, she gets on the Seventh Avenue bus. 9:40, she gets off the bus at Fortieth Street and walks across to the Port Authority Terminal on Eighth Avenue. 10:00, Cindy's watching her in the terminal. That's the latest we've got."

Hull hung up the microphone and shook his head, puzzled. "You figure she's going to take a bus all the way back to Texas?"

"Without her baggage and without checking out of the hotel?"

"There you go, presuming innocence again."

"I spent a day with her. She's not a deadbeat. She wouldn't duck out of the hotel without paying her bill."

"I hope you're right. Otherwise Shepard's going to rack up a hell of a travel and overtime chit."

The radio sputtered and crackled. Hull picked up the microphone. "Go ahead."

"Latest word from Cindy is that the Tobin girl picked up a timetable from New England Coastal Bus Lines and left the terminal."

"What do you make of that?" Hull asked Wade.

"She's not going back to Texas on the bus, that's for sure."

"Lloyd, you're the only one she's come in contact with so far whom she trusts. I want you to take advantage of that."

Wade frowned.

"What's the matter with you young guys?" Hull asked plaintively. "She's a good-looking broad. When I was your age, I'd have jumped at that kind of duty. Get in touch with her. Stay close to her. Can you do that in some natural kind of way?"

"The most natural way in the world. I'm the family minister, remember?" he asked bitterly.

"How could I forget? I ordained you."

Chapter 25

Wheeler felt the hand on his shoulder and sensed that he was in trouble.

"I'm afraid you've broken a cardinal rule."

Wheeler shook himself awake and blinked. "What's that?" A delaying action while he pulled his head together. He knew what the man must be talking about.

"Sleeping in the lobby."

"Oh! That." He brushed the offense away with a flick of his hand. Now he remembered where he was—in the lobby of The Brittany—and his gentle persecutor was the man who'd been behind the desk when he took up his vigil—he glanced at his watch—nearly an hour ago at ten o'clock. He bent over and picked up the sheets of the newspaper that had slid off his lap onto the floor. "I was just resting my eyes. My glasses are in for repair and I have to ease up the strain now and then."

"You were snoring, sir. It's somewhat disturbing of the peace."

"Thanks. I'll be all right now." Damn! he thought. How did Maitland expect him to function? He hadn't had a decent night's sleep in three days.

"May I ask your room number, sir?" Cagey guy. Didn't want to offend a paying customer.

"I'm waiting for one of the guests." She might have walked right past him while he was nodding.

"You've been waiting for the better part of an hour, sir." And Wheeler thought he had been unobtrusive.

"Ah! There she is now." Thank God! He saw Andrea coming through the revolving door. She was carrying a small brown manila envelope, and she headed straight for the desk.

Wheeler started across the lobby, glancing back once. The manager was still watching him. He hoped Andrea would greet him with some sign of recognition; otherwise he foresaw another unpleasant night in jail. For vagrancy.

At the desk Andrea picked up her keys and a small folded message form. The message was from Lloyd Wade, asking her to call him. She told the clerk she was expecting a special delivery letter later in the day and that she wanted to be notified immediately upon its arrival. She slipped the message from Wade into her coat pocket, turned, and started toward the elevators, almost colliding with Wheeler.

"Hi, Sis!" He smiled at her ingenuously.

For a moment she looked puzzled. Then she simply said: "It's you." Not the warmest greeting in the world, but at least she hadn't screamed. "How did you know to find me here?"

Wheeler shrugged. "I asked at the other hotel. They told

152

me you'd come here. C'mon. There's a coffee shop at the other end of the lobby. Let's sit down and talk." He took her by the arm and started guiding her across the lobby. He caught a glimpse of the manager, who, apparently satisfied, squared his shoulders and strolled off to attend to another lobby lounger. Fortunately, the manager's back was turned when Andrea shook off Wheeler's guiding hand.

"What do you mean, you asked at the other hotel? I never even told you I was staying there."

"I was anxious to see you, Sis."

"That doesn't answer my question."

"Look, Sis," he said cajolingly.

"And stop calling me 'Sis.' "

"What do you want me to call you?"

"I don't want you to call me anything. I just want you to go away."

"Okay! Just give me a few minutes. I know we weren't the best friends in the world, but you'd think after all these years . . . and with Dad gone . . . and . . . "

"Oh! Come on!" Andrea snapped.

"Come on, what?"

Andrea shrugged, resigned. "Come on. Let's have a cup of coffee."

Wheeler grinned, sincerely grateful, and followed her across the lobby toward the coffee shop. He would figure out, once they were there, how he could get a look at what she had in that manila envelope.

On the mezzanine balcony that ringed the lobby and doubled as a cocktail lounge, Lenny Blue sat, grimly sipping a beer, his eyes riveted on the exchange taking place below between Andrea and Wheeler. He lowered his stein and patted the foam from his lip, the scar glowing angry red. He too was interested in what she was carrying in the manila envelope.

When Andrea and Wheeler came out of the coffee shop fifteen minutes later, the manila envelope wasn't anywhere in sight. From his table on the mezzanine Lenny Blue watched them cross the lobby together and stand for a moment near the elevators, watched Andrea step into the first elevator to arrive, watched the man cross to the back of the lobby where the bank of telephones was situated. Lenny paid for his drinks and stood up. He was pretty sure of what had become of the envelope. She had passed it to the guy when they were in the coffee shop.

Down in the lobby Wheeler got through to Maitland.
"Where are you calling from?" Maitland asked.
"The hotel."
"That's a relief."
"Spare me, please. I'm dead on my feet."
"Did you speak to her?"
"Yeah."
"Well?"
"Either she isn't willing to let bygones be bygones, or she smells a rat. She sure as hell didn't unburden herself to me. I don't think this approach is going to work at all. Once I thought I had her going. Something I said made her remember an Aunt Jane."
"Aunt who?"
"Aunt Jane."
"I don't have anything on Aunt Jane."
"There's probably a lot you don't have. Aunt Jane must

154

have been one of the few bright spots in the kid's life, from the way she talked. Anyway, all I could do was nod and grunt, and then she clammed up on me. She just nodded and grunted from then on in. Maybe if we'd had something on this Aunt Jane, something I could talk about, I could have kept her open. In fact, I had a feeling that whatever I was doing or saying was amusing her immensely. She's no patty-cake, that girl.

"She was carrying an envelope that looked interesting, so I brushed it off the table with my elbow to see if I could sneak a peak. It wasn't sealed, just held shut with a clasp. Well, I fumbled around down there and just got it open when her head's down there under the table with mine and she's holding out her hand for the envelope and giving me a glib 'thank you.' She locked it up in her purse after that, pretty damn pointedly, I think, and I didn't get another shot at it. Maybe you'll want someone to check out her room or dip into her bag later."

"A kind of brownish manila envelope?" Maitland asked. "Maybe four by five?"

"That sounds like it."

"Forget it. She picked up some bus schedules a little while ago and they threw in a couple of tourist come-ons. That's what's in the envelope."

"Why the hell didn't someone tell me?"

"If you'd made your half-hour check-in, someone would have."

Wheeler let it drop. He didn't want to explain that he'd been dozing through his half-hour check-in. "Listen. Am I off duty now?" he asked. "I've got to get home and get some sleep."

"Pleasant dreams," Maitland said.

Wheeler shuffled across the lobby, hands deep in pockets, head down. He got a cab outside.

Lenny Blue got into a cab right behind him.

Andrea opened the door to her room and left it wide open. Then she checked the bathroom and the closet; she even knelt down and looked under the bed, feeling foolish, like some high-strung Victorian spinster. She satisfied herself that there was no one in the room. Then she went back and shut the door and locked it.

She set her purse down on the dresser, hung up her coat, took a deep breath, and went over to her suitcase on the little stand at the foot of the bed. She hunkered down and examined the zipper, and knew she wasn't losing her mind. Someone had been in her room and had gone through her things. When she had left after breakfast, she had zipped the case almost all the way shut, but not quite. She had left the zipper tab in a position about half an inch from the end of its track. She had counted the open teeth. There had been seven. Whoever had opened her bag had neatly shut it all the way.

She opened the suitcase and took inventory of her things. Everything was just as she had left it. She counted her traveler's checks. They were all there.

The things she had put in the dresser drawer also appeared undisturbed, though she was sure that the dresser must have been investigated, too.

She dropped down into a chair and nibbled reflectively on a thumbnail. She could feel her heart hammering at an alarming pace.

"Damn!" she shouted at the disinterested walls. "Damn!" She picked up the ashtray from the little table beside her and hurled it across the room at nothing in particular. It thumped into the quilted headboard of the bed and dropped harmlessly onto the pillow. She felt better. She was breathing faster, but her heart had stopped its hammering. She blew out a long breath and began to pace back and forth in front of the bed. She could call the police, but to what purpose? No crime had been committed. She could change hotels again. But what good would that do? Whoever was interested in her would find her again, as they had today. She couldn't change hotels now anyway. She was expecting that letter. If it came by 3:00 or even 3:30, she could catch the 4:10 bus. If it came after that, there was a bus at 11:30 that night. But it might not even arrive by then, in which case she'd have to spend another night here. She felt she had to talk to someone or she'd go out of her mind.

She went to the dresser and emptied out her purse, searching for the message Lloyd Wade had left. Frenetically, she sifted through the coins and cards, tubes of makeup and combs, useless addresses and old supermarket receipts, and it wasn't there. Then she remembered and went to the closet and found it in her coat pocket where she had thrust it when the man who claimed to be her brother had approached her in the lobby.

Chapter

26

The little lucite buttons on the call director console were winking. The receptionist mechanically snuffed them out one by one with a gaudily beringed forefinger as she transferred the incoming inquiries to their destinations. She hesitated a moment before dealing with the fourth button down on the left and raised a penciled eyebrow. She had taped a piece of white adhesive beside that button as a reminder. She tapped the button down and spoke solemnly into the mouthpiece: "Vicarage."

"May I speak to Reverend Wade, please, if he's there?" A female voice. Troubled.

"One moment, please. I'll see if we can locate him." She tapped down the hold button and buzzed Lloyd Wade's desk. "I think I have your call here."

Lloyd Wade was sitting at the end of a double row of formica-topped sheet metal

158

desks that looked like a two-lane traffic jam. He clapped his hand close to his free ear to shut out the clatter of the surrounding typewriters.

"Put her on hold for a minute. Make out like you had to hunt me down. Then switch her into Hull's office. I'll take it in there. This place sounds like a tool and die works."

He hung up his phone and moved quickly to the back of the bullpen. Hull's door was open, but he tapped on it anyway to get Hull's attention. Hull was leaning across his desk, staring morosely out at nothing. A typescript folder was lying open on the desk in front of him: the transcript of the meeting between Sturdivant, Maitland, and himself.

"Can I use your office for a little while?" Wade asked.

"Why? You want to impress some broad?"

"Something like that."

"Her?" he asked hopefully. Wade nodded.

Hull hauled himself out of his chair. "Make it good. The next guy in here may not be as congenial as I am."

"What's the matter?" Wade asked, crossing over behind the desk. He glanced down at the open page in the folder.

"Just had a call from Washington," Hull replied. "Crockett is not only snapping out of it, he's snapping out in high style. No aphasia, no serious paralyses. Just a little trouble with his left hand. He'll be seeing visitors tomorrow. He may be out of the hospital in a week. Unless we short-circuit that file of his, we're all liable to be out on the street." Hull became aware that he had left the folder open. He reached across the desk and flipped it shut. "Sorry. For my eyes only." But Wade had already read part of one of the more disturbingly venal exchanges.

Wade picked up the phone. "Put her through, now, please."

Click, dead line, *click,* Andrea's voice, "Reverend Wade?"

"Speaking."

"Lloyd, this is Andrea Tobin." She sounded ill at ease. "I had a message that you'd called."

"Oh! Yes." He replied with clerical joviality. "Nothing special. Just like to keep track of my—uh—flock. How are you doing today?"

She started hesitantly. "Well . . . the truth is . . . there's something I'd like to talk to you about." And finished in a rush, "Can I come down to see you?"

Wade looked out through the glass panel in Hull's door and shook his head. "No. I think it would be better if I came to see you. Have you had lunch yet?"

"No."

"I'll meet you in your lobby in a half hour." He put the phone down, turned to Hull and sighed heavily. "Well, there's the answer to your prayers: a soul in search of a confessor." He started for the elevator.

"In that case," Hull called after him, "don't forget your collar."

Wade did a sharp about-face and turned back toward his locker.

Chapter 27

It took courage, or maybe desperation, for them to stand out there day after day in the damp cold, the balloon man with his tank of compressed air, the pretzel vendor with his cart and basket, stomping their feet, beating their chapped hands together for warmth. Eyes watering, noses blue. With so few people in the park and the winter-shortened days, Andrea wondered how they could make the price of a meal and lodging by nightfall.

Wade couldn't help wondering if they hadn't been planted there by Maitland or Sturdivant, or both.

He and Andrea were sitting in the cozy warmth of the glassed-in terrace of the Parks Department restaurant overlooking the quadrangle of the zoo. The black-barred cages along both sides of the square were empty and lifeless. The big cats and monkeys, the chimps and the

161

birds that lolled and climbed and dozed and flew about there in warmer weather had been shut off inside the heated buildings. Only an occasional baleful moan or echoing growl signaled the fact that they were still in residence. But the seals were having the time of their lives in the frigid water in the open pool at the center of the square, the only living things in sight that Wade found himself able to view without suspicion. Slippery, slick, and glistening wet, they dove and splashed and streaked about, barking jubilantly, free of the daily nuisance of demanding summertime crowds.

Wade poked thoughtfully at the baked beans on his plate as Andrea related her experience of the previous night: the man in the tub who had vanished. Wade knew what had happened to him, but there was no way he could tell her. What could he tell her?

"You mustn't forget, Andrea . . . you had just lost your father. You may have been more distraught than you realized." A crock of bull.

"Did I imagine those three men who showed up at the cemetery? You saw them too, Lloyd."

"I saw them."

"The man in my room last night was one of those three. The man who bought me coffee this morning was another one. Do you know why I even allowed myself to sit down and talk to him?" Wade shook his head no. "Because there was a residue of doubt in my mind yesterday. Maybe my brother did have that scar removed. Maybe one of those three was my brother.

"So I sat down with him and let him tell me about old times. He knew a good deal about us, and I was almost beginning to believe him. And then I thought I'd remind him about our Aunt Jane, of whom we were both so fond; in fact, our fondness for Aunt Jane was the only thing we really shared as kids. And he agreed about Aunt Jane. And then I knew for sure he was a phony. We never had an Aunt Jane."

Wade sighed. The girl was scared, and he had been sent there to take advantage of her vulnerability. He hated himself for it.

"I'm sorry," he heard her saying. "I have no right to saddle you with this."

Wade shook his head. He had grown to detest his job.

"It's my problem," she said. "I should be able to handle it."

Wade placed a restraining hand on her arm. He knew that Andrea was in more danger than she realized and that she couldn't handle it by herself. "Andrea, you seem to think that somebody is trying to get to you . . . "

"I don't think. I know!"

"All right. Why?"

She looked away, at the seals, at the balloon man.

"Andrea! You've got to let me help you." Well, he thought, that's about the neatest rationale for betrayal I've managed in a long time.

"Forget I said anything, Lloyd."

"Was it something your father left you?"

"My father had practically no personal possessions."

"Then, think! You must have something these people want, something worth all the trouble and risk they are putting themselves to, because they must be incurring risks, you know."

She didn't respond. She just shook her head slowly from side to side, either refuting his suggestion or trying to shake off the discomfort his probing was causing her.

He tried a different approach. "Andrea, maybe you have nothing that they could possibly want . . . " She nodded slowly in agreement. "Maybe they only *think* you have something they want . . . . " The look of relief that came over her face was so moving that he wished he could let it go at that. He took a deep breath and blew apart the frail fabric of her self-deception.

"But Andrea, whether you actually *have* something they want . . . or whether they only *think* you do, makes no difference. In fact, not having it may bring you more pain than having it. If you *have* it, you can give it up at your option. If you don't have it at all, they may hurt and hurt you because they can't afford to let themselves believe that you don't. They'll keep hammering at you until there's nothing left to hammer at, and only then will they be satisfied that maybe you were telling the truth in the first place."

Her eyes were locked on his, narrowed and painfully comprehending, her lips just slightly parted, forming an unspoken question. Wade knew that he had blundered. He tried to change the subject before her thoughts could coalesce. She just kept boring into him with eyes that looked betrayed. Wade knew it was too late, but he struggled on. "Well, they might think your father had some knowledge of some of Crockett's most sensitive material and that maybe he had passed it on to you."

"How would you know all that?" she asked, her voice flat, dead, devoid of any emotion.

He shrugged defensively. "You told me yourself about your father working for Crockett."

"I don't mean about my father and Crockett. I mean, how do you know so much about pursuit and interrogation? You sound like a man who's had personal experience. How does a missionary minister come to know such things firsthand?"

He put a hand placatingly on hers. She pulled her hand away. "It's a bit late for the laying on of hands."

"Andrea," he pleaded with her, "you're a little over-wrought."

"The hell I am. I'm a lot overwrought. I've been lied to, tricked, deceived, and conned by damn near everyone I've come in contact with for the past three days, and most of all by you. Who do you belong to, Lloyd? If that's your name." She shoved her chair back, its metal legs scraping clangorously across the flagstone floor, and then tilting and toppling with a crash. She didn't stop to pick it up, but strode angrily off the terrace. A blue-haired old woman sipping hot chocolate near the door gave her a conspiratorial wink and an encouraging upraised fist as she passed. Wade righted the toppled chair and ran after her. He caught up with her halfway down the line of empty monkey cages.

"Andrea," he confessed, "I lied to you."

"What else is new?" She kept walking, eyes straight ahead, past the row of cages, past the huddled pretzel vendor, onto the path that went around the old turreted nineteenth-century arsenal building that fronted the zoo, up the flight of shallow stone steps that led out onto Fifth Avenue.

Wade took the steps two at a time and confronted her at the top. "You asked who I belong to!"

For reply she slammed the palm of her hand against his shoulder and spun him aside. She made a dash for the bus pulling into the stop zone half a block away. There were three or four school kids climbing aboard wielding briefcases and flashing school passes. She made it. But Wade was right behind her. They stood pressed together side by side in the crowded aisle, hanging onto the overhead grips to keep from being thrown by the lurching and pitching of the vehicle.

"I can't tell you here," he whispered in desperate apology. "It's too crowded."

She didn't reply. She worked her way up the aisle toward the center door, Wade worming his way along behind her, and got off across from Tiffany's at Fifty-seventh Street.

Wade kept pace with her as she strode north, past Bergdorf's, around the Pulitzer Fountain, and then headed for Central Park South. As they passed in front of the huge equestrian statue of General Sherman, Wade glanced around, assured himself that no one was within earshot and blurted, "I'm GSC." He stopped and waited for the initials to work their magic. To his astonishment Andrea stepped off the curb and crossed the street without so much as a hitch in her stride. "But that doesn't mean I don't have your best interests at heart." Wade ran after her, adroitly dodging hansom cabs and Cadillacs while he pleaded his case.

"We have reason to believe your father walked off with some very sensitive material." She continued to stride swiftly up Central Park South, past the side door of the Plaza Hotel and the glowering totems bolted into the sidewalk outside Trader Vic's. "I've been ordered to do my best to see that it doesn't fall into the wrong hands."

A delivery boy riding a three-wheeled pedal-cart like it was Demolition Derby Day came zigzagging down the sidewalk, where he had no right to be in the first place, warning pedestrians out of the way with mad, shrill whistles and cursing in Spanish those who held their ground and forced him to swerve. Andrea held her ground. Wade ducked aside and then caught up.

"If you want to condemn me for trying to do my job, that's your prerogative. But you've got to believe me when I say that, above all, I don't want to see you hurt. There are other

166

people looking for that material, and I don't know what they'd do to get it."

She turned sharply and spun through the revolving door of her hotel. He turned to follow, slammed into the blue-coated doorman, did a little two-step right and left and finally got around. He pushed through the door and impotently watched her retreating across the lobby toward the elevators. With the part of his mind that belonged to himself and not to the service, he silently wished her luck.

There was nothing more he could do. He had gone as far as to expose the mission and blow his cover without authorization, and he'd have to answer for that. Dejectedly he began padding across the thick pile of the lobby carpet toward the bank of public phones to call Hull and let him know that unless he could decide on a new approach or, God forbid, on a show of force, the mission was as good as scrubbed.

Out of the corner of his eye he caught the movement of the elevator door opening and two or three people coming out. He stopped to watch her as she stepped inside, and then, out of nowhere, as the door began to close, he saw the man slip in behind her, and as the man faced front just before the doors slid shut, he thought he saw an upper lip cleft by a scar.

He threaded his way quickly across the lobby, keeping his eyes on the light indicator above the elevator doors. He knew that her room was on the sixth floor, but that was no guarantee that they would get off there. The little white lights winked on and off at two, on and off at three, on and off at four. He pressed urgently on the call button that would bring the other elevator down. The damned thing was programmed to take its own sweet time. On and off went the little light on five. And then something went wrong. Six didn't light up. Wade guessed what must have happened. The bastard had thrown the emergency stop and stalled the elevator between floors. And he had Andrea there. Wade left the elevator bank and ran for the service stairs.

But Wade had guessed wrong. It had been Andrea, not her brother, who had stopped the elevator between floors.

She stepped into the elevator, seething over Wade's deceit, and pressed the button for her floor. She stood before the panel of buttons on the wall, occupied with her thoughts, waiting for the doors to shut.

She was aware, just as the doors began to close, that someone had joined her in the car: a man, and, for an angry instant, she thought it must be Wade. She turned on him, prepared to lash out. Her eyes went wide in astonishment; her jaw dropped. She looked to the doors, but they had closed, shutting off escape into the busy lobby. With a little bounce and tug, the elevator began its regulated ascent.

Her brother didn't smile, didn't greet her effusively, didn't bend to kiss her cheek as the phonies had done. He was the real thing. He stood stolidly across from her, his face expressionless, his eyes emotionless, licking at the scar on his lip with his tongue. The elevator passed the mezzanine. She prayed that somewhere, before it reached her floor, it would stop, that someone would get on.

"What have you done with them, Andy?"

"I don't have them." The elevator passed the first floor.

"Don't lie to me."

The elevator passed the second floor.

"Remember how I used to play with you when we were kids?" She remembered, and the memory made her shudder.

168

"I've learned a few new tricks. I'll show you when we get to your room." She looked away from him, and her eye fell on the two red buttons, side by side, at the top of the pane. ALARM and EMERGENCY STOP. The elevator was passing five. She raised her hand as if to smooth down her hair. Then she thrust it out, quickly, thumb poised to hit the alarm button.

But Lenny was quicker than she was; she'd forgotten how quick. He caught her wrist and deflected her thrust. Her thumb missed the alarm button as he twisted her arm, throwing her sideways and off balance. The back of her upraised fist smashed into the EMERGENCY STOP. They were momentarily lifted up on their toes by the abrupt loss of motion. The elevator quivered, and then there was no movement at all. It hung dead in its shaft, halfway between the fifth and sixth floors.

"Bitch!" He sent her hurtling against the back wall of the car. He stood across from her, legs planted wide, head down, breathing hard, his nostrils spitting tiny jets of moisture.

He began stabbing at the buttons on the callboard in a frenzied attempt to start the car moving again. The elevator didn't respond. Agitated as he was, she hoped that he wouldn't notice the small lettering around the outer ring of the button: "Push to stop. Pull to start." Scared as she was, she sensed that she had a better chance here than in her room. The stalled elevator was almost as good as an alarm. Someone was bound to come. He gave up and turned to her again. "We'll see how smart you are."

She knew that he was capable of inflicting pain. But pain was something she could get over. Death was another thing entirely. She didn't think he'd kill her until she told him what he wanted to know. And he wouldn't have time to hurt her

169

badly enough to make her tell before someone arrived. She stood outside herself, monitoring her thoughts, and was amazed that she could think logically at all.

He reached into his pocket and flicked out a gravity knife. He held the stainless steel blade up at eye level, the handle gripped almost daintily between thumb and index finger, like someone at a cocktail party offering a toast.

She knew it would be futile to fight him. He was bigger, heavier, stronger than she. She would only enrage him and perhaps precipitate a fatal accident.

He took a step toward her, and she slipped along the back wall until she found herself wedged in the corner.

He was only inches away from her now, the knife blade aimed at a point on her cheek just below her right eye. She took a deep breath and employed the only weapon she had at her disposal. She rolled her eyes up, emitted a little sigh, and slid to the floor in a faint.

Wade arrived on the sixth floor, gasping. He sagged against the wall across from the elevator doors hoping that if the car was stuck, it would stay stuck for a few seconds longer. If the door opened now, he knew he would be absolutely useless.

He lurched across the vestibule and leaned on the call buttons, both up and down, with his outstretched palm, just to be doing something while he caught his breath. He knew that if the elevator was stalled, this wouldn't get it started again. He also knew that elevators have escape hatches in their ceilings. If he could pry the doors open, he could get down into the car through the hatch.

He worked his fingers between the rubber lips that padded the leading edges of the sliding doors and managed to part them enough so that he could see a little way into the shaft.

His view straight ahead was blocked by the big iron handle of the elbow-jointed bar by means of which the door could be opened manually from inside the shaft. Directing his eyes down, he saw the top of the elevator about three feet below the level of the sixth floor.

He tried to hold the rubber lip open with his left hand while he forced his right hand through. If he could manage to get a grip on the handle of the bar, he might be able to work the door open manually. But the space was too restricted. He managed to get his hand through as far as the wrist, managed even to curl his fingers around the handle, but the pressure of the rubber against his tendons and muscles was so great that he was unable to exert the necessary downward force. He needed a crowbar, a jimmy, a piece of iron pipe, something narrow in circumference and rigid and strong that he could use as a lever.

At the far end of the corridor he saw a bright red fire extinguisher hanging from a bracket on the wall, and, hanging above it, a long-handled axe.

"Oh, shee-it," she heard her brother groan disgustedly, and she knew she had bought herself a little time. After all, how do you deal with a subject who has just passed out on you?

In the dead silence inside the car she heard a click. She hoped it was the knife being folded up and put away.

The car shook a little as he knelt over her. She could feel his knee pressing against her thigh, feel his breath against her face.

"Come on, Andy!" A hoarse, urgent whisper, like a jockey importuning his mount.

Mentally she prepared herself for the slap that was bound

to come. It wouldn't be too hard—his intent would be to bring her around rather than send her into a coma—but it would sting, and she would have to exert every ounce of will power she possessed to remain limp, to keep from crying out or wincing or in any way betraying the fact that she was conscious.

She felt his hands like the steel tines of a forklift forcing their way under her armpits. She felt her torso being raised by a force, relentless and impersonal. She let her hands and arms hang limp. He propped her up in the corner in a sitting position, her legs straight out in front. Her head lolled forward onto her chest. He gripped her chin with strong fingers and raised it.

"Andrea!" he rasped commandingly.

Then the slap came, across her left cheek, stunning and sharp as if a leather strap had been brought into play, and it caught her by surprise. With all the lifting and shifting of her body she had forgotten that she should have been expecting it: a slap delivered by a practiced hand, expertly measured, productive of a clean, localized, almost exquisite pain. An almost irresistible stimulant. Silvery flashes behind her eyes, like sunlight glinting off mica. She had no way of knowing whether she had betrayed herself by a blink or a grimace.

Was he studying her face? He still held her chin in his left hand; it must be the left, because he had struck her with the right.

"Andrea!" He struck her again, the same kind of carefully directed blow. Only the effect wasn't as stunning, because the cheek was starting to go numb.

He let her chin drop, and she knew she hadn't given herself away.

There was the sound of a click. Had he opened the knife

again? She could feel the blood draining from her head, and she wondered if she really was going to faint. Surely someone must have noticed by now that the elevator was out of order.

She heard a shuffling and scraping a couple of feet to her left on the floor, where she had let her purse drop. The click had been the sound of her purse as he'd snapped it open. He was going through her things. The clink of coins, the rattle of paper. He would find nothing. A thud. He tossed the purse into a corner.

The car began to bounce and shudder as if he were jumping in place. Once, twice, three times. Then it became still again. She could hear shoes scraping against the inside of the wall at about the level of her head, but in the opposite corner of the car, like a monkey climbing around a cage. She wondered if he had gone berserk. If he had, there was no predicting what he might do to her, conscious or unconscious. Swelling waves of panic battered at her foundering resolve. She was seized by an almost overwhelming need to release herself from the terrors of her self-imposed blindness, to open her eyes and see.

She heard a protracted harsh metallic scrape somewhere in the ceiling overhead, followed by a change in ambiance, a lessening of the stultifying feeling of airlessness within the car, as if a window had been opened. Then she knew what he had done. He had climbed onto the brass handrail that ran waist-high around the inside of the elevator. Using that as a step, he had reached up and slid open the escape hatch in the ceiling of the car. She could hear the hum of machinery in the shaft. Perhaps he planned to climb out through the top and force the door on the floor above. Perhaps he would leave. Please, God!

There was a thud and the car shuddered again. He had dropped back down.

Her chin was gripped in his hand again. "Come on, Andy!" Anger added to the urgency in his voice. The slap. A little harder, but still carefully placed and controlled. The slap again. Above the ringing din inside her head, she heard the crackle and sputter of a small loudspeaker.

"You passengers in the elevator. Don't panic. You are in no immediate danger." Andrea didn't know whether to laugh or cry. It was the hotel manager using the emergency intercom connected to the lobby. "We know you've stalled and have sent for a repair crew. But you may be able to help yourselves. Guests have occasionally mistaken the emergency stop button for one of the floors. Look at the emergency stop button. It is the red button at the top of the right-hand column. Is it depressed? If it is, then you need only pull it toward you to restart the elevator. You passengers in the elevator. Don't panic." He was starting the whole spiel again, like a recording.

"Okay, Andy." Lenny had gotten the message. The following slap was hard and uncontrolled and caught her on the cheekbone. She remained immobile.

"Goddammit, I'll wake you up!" She braced herself. But no slap came. She began counting off the seconds. Maybe he was going to restart the car and then carry her to her room.

She was hit in the face by a stream of water, its manifestation so startling that involuntarily she jerked her head. She hurled herself out of the way, sputtering and gagging. She wiped her face with the back of her hand and looked up appalled.

He was grinning savagely, just like when they were kids. "Never fails!"

"You bastard," she gasped.

He zipped up his fly. "Now let's get out of here."

He dragged her to her feet with one hand and reached up with the other and pulled the emergency stop button toward him. The car began to rise.

A weight like a falling body thumped down heavily onto the roof over their heads. She looked up and saw Lloyd Wade's face peering down through the half-open hatch in the ceiling.

Lenny saw him, too, just as the elevator stopped again, this time at the sixth floor.

"Hold it! Right where you are!" But his ability to back up his command with strong and immediate action was questionable. The strong voice seemed to be coming from a disembodied head floating in the shaft above the ceiling. The elevator doors slid open and Lenny Blue took off.

By the time Wade had pushed the hatch back far enough to give himself shoulder room and had dropped down into the car, the doors had shut again. The elevator was on its way up to the next floor, since Lenny had programmed that into the machinery when he had tried futilely to restart the car by pressing every button in sight just a couple of minutes earlier.

"Thanks again," said Andrea gratefully. "What have I done to deserve you?"

"That your brother?" Wade asked.

Andrea nodded.

"I guess we've lost him," Wade said dejectedly.

"Let's hope for another twelve years, at least."

Wade agreed. "It didn't look like a family scene by Norman Rockwell." Then he noticed her hair. "What happened? Did a sprinkler go off or something?"

"Something," she conceded. "Yeah. Something." Her body convulsed and she began to cry.

The elevator stopped and Wade helped her out.

"Where are we?" she asked, sniffling back her tears. She began searching her purse for a Kleenex.

Wade looked at the number printed on the inner face of the doorpost. "Nine." Wade handed her his handkerchief. "It's clean."

She blew her nose heartily. "It's not clean anymore. Sorry."

They started down the stairs to the sixth floor.

"Lloyd," she asked, "would you mind staying with me a little while?"

"Of course not."

"There's something I want to talk to you about. But there's something I absolutely have to do first."

"Have a nice stiff drink?"

"No. A nice hot shower." She blew her nose again.

Chapter 28

She came out of the shower looking dewy and delicious, wrapped in a coral-colored terrycloth robe, her head wrapped turban-style in one of the hotel towels. Her face was invitingly flushed from the warmth of the water. Her bare legs glowed pink from her knees to her toes. She looked very much as if she had just made love.

"Any visitors?" she asked.

"No."

She noticed the way he was looking at her and said: "Maybe I'd better get dressed." She started toward the closet.

"Please!" Wade stopped her. "You had something you wanted to talk about."

"Yeah," she said, and sat down in a chair across from him. "There seem to be a lot of guys around who are bigger and heavier and a lot more expert in the martial arts than I am, and I think I need a little help."

"I thought you'd never ask."

"What'll it cost me?"

"Crockett's files."

"I can't do that. My father wanted them returned to Mr. Crockett or destroyed."

"He didn't figure on your brother."

Andrea stood up and began pacing. "I wish I had a license to carry a gun."

Wade smiled. "You feel like shooting me?"

"Why would I want to shoot you? You're the only decent person I've met since I came here. Who are all those other people anyway?"

"They belong to other agencies. A lot of very highly placed individuals have a personal interest in those files."

"Give me a cigarette, will you?"

"I didn't know you smoked."

"I don't, except when I'm thinking."

He held his coat open for her to see. "I don't smoke at all."

She picked up the phone, asked for room service, and ordered a package of cigarettes, anything mild. She cupped her hand over the phone and asked Wade if he wanted a hamburger.

"Does that help you think, too?"

"I didn't finish my lunch, remember?"

"Neither did I, come to think of it," Wade said.

She ordered hamburgers and Cokes. Then she cupped her hand over the phone and turned to Wade again. "They don't have hamburgers. Only chopped sirloin on toast. Is that all right?"

"That's all right."

She gave the order and hung up. "What's the difference

between hamburger and chopped sirloin?" she asked Wade.

"About a buck and a half."

Andrea crossed the room and dropped back into her chair. Her robe fell open at the knee as she crossed her legs, and she noticed the way Wade was looking at her. She got up again. "I think I will get dressed. You look to me like a man at the losing end of a moral battle, *Reverend* Wade." She took some clothes out of the closet and locked herself in the bathroom.

Wade got out of his chair and moved the drapes aside so he could look out the window. The hotel advertised panoramic views of Central Park, but her room faced onto a courtyard, walled in by grimy white brick. High-priced squalor. He let the drapes fall.

"Do you know what your brother wants with the file?" he called through the bathroom door.

"Maybe he wants to bring down the house. That's all he's really ever wanted. Our house when we were kids . . . everyone's house now. It's all the same to him."

When she came out of the bathroom, she looked business-like in slacks and a shirt. The towel was still wrapped around her head. "You know," she said, "I've been thinking about those files." She began turning on the lamps in the room. The gloomy light filtering in from the courtyard was almost gone. "I think maybe it's too risky to try to return them to Mr. Crockett. I think maybe my father did us all a favor when he took them. I think maybe I just ought to follow the second part of his instructions and destroy them. Maybe we'll all be a lot better off." She looked at Wade inquisitively.

"You want me to help you destroy them?" he asked incredulously.

"Why not? That way you're sure nobody else will get control of the files to your agency's disadvantage."

"That's a whole new ball game. I'd need authorization."

"From whom?"

"My controller would have to call his director in Washington. I don't think he'd go for it."

"Why not? Everybody will wind up even."

"That's just it. Why settle for 'even' when, for a little risk, you might wind up with an advantage?"

"Try."

Wade picked up the phone and called Hull. When he hung up, he looked troubled. "He said to tell you he'll accept losing the files rather than risk the chance of somebody else getting them first."

"But you said he'd have to check with Washington first."

"Yeah."

"There's a catch?"

"Always. The reason he didn't check with Washington was that he didn't even think the proposition worth considering."

"But you just said he would accept . . . "

"That's what he told me to tell you. But when you pick up that file I'm supposed to make damn sure you *don't* destroy it."

Andrea studied him with concern. "You just breached agency security."

"Uh-huh." He looked away, trying to avoid her eyes.

"Why?"

Wade shrugged. "Maybe I'm ready for a career change."

"I can't let you blow your career on my account."

"Maybe it's not just on your account. Now, let's go, before someone decides to ride shotgun on the shotgun rider."

180

Andrea looked discomposed. "We can't."
"Why not?"
"Because I don't know where it is . . . yet."

Chapter

29

Wade stared at her, dumbfounded. "What do you mean, you don't know where it is?"

There was a polite knock at the door.

"Who's there?" she called out.

"Room service."

She reached for the doorknob, but Wade grabbed her wrist. "Wait a minute."

"It's only room service."

"And I'm a minister of the gospel. Haven't you learned anything these past three days?" He flattened himself against the wall on the blind side of the door, took hold of the knob, and turned it slowly until he felt the catch release; then he yanked the door open with a jerk. The man waiting outside was thoroughly startled.

"You did order something from room service, didn't you?" he asked Andrea, nonplused.

She nodded. "Come right in."

He came in as warily as if he were entering a mine field, rolling his cart before him and shifting his eyes right and left.

Wade stepped out from behind the door and announced: "I'll take care of him." The waiter blanched. "The bill," Wade explained.

"Oh! . . . yes . . . of course." He fumbled a pencil out of his pocket and held the bill out for signature. "$9.05."

"For two hamburgers and two Cokes and a pack of cigarettes?" Andrea protested.

"I'm sorry, ma'am," he said weakly. "Would you like me to take them back?"

Wade handed him a ten-dollar bill.

"Cash?" the man asked in disbelief.

"Cash. Keep the change."

"Just leave the cart in the hall when you're through." He beat a hasty retreat, closing the door carefully behind him.

"You scared hell out of the poor man."

"He'll recover. I think I overtipped him."

"Ten percent?"

"Oh." His face fell. "I never could do decimals. Now, what about those files?"

"I told you, I don't know yet."

"Then what have we been wasting our time for?" His voice began to rise.

"Don't yell at me. I don't like to be yelled at."

Wade turned away from her and propped one hand against the wall. He groaned.

"And none of those damned patronizing groans, either, if you please."

"Forgive me, I'm a sexist."

"A what!"

"Never mind."

"What is it with you men?" She turned away, annoyed. "I'm going to have my hamburger before it gets cold."

He whirled on her. "What do you mean, you don't know . . . yet? Either you know or you don't know. If you don't know now, who's going to tell you?"

"My father." He looked at her incredulously. "He sent me a card just before he had his accident. I've asked my post office to forward it. It may be here this evening. You're welcome to wait if you want to." She lifted the lid off one of the dishes on the cart and made a face. "Chopped sirloin."

"That's me," Wade said. He pulled a couple of chairs up to the cart.

They began to eat the hamburgers, cutting them up with knives and forks. "Hell of a way to eat a hamburger," she complained.

"Here!" he said, spearing his toast with his fork. "Put this on top of yours and then you can eat it properly."

"You're very generous." She took his toast and laid it on top of her hamburger, picked the whole greasy sandwich up in her hands and began gnawing away at it. "What a mess."

"The sirloin?"

"Everything."

He watched her munching away at the chopped sirloin and sipping her Coke, and he thought how nice it would be if he were just a guy and she was just a girl and a hamburger was a hamburger and the world wasn't one big ripoff arena with people climbing all over each other with the questionable objective of being king of the hill for a little while until someone else climbed up and knocked them off. It was a kid's game carried to murderous lengths by grownups who

184

had lost sight of the fact that it was no more than a game after all. Nothing was.

"You're not married, are you?" he asked.

"No."

"How come?"

"What do you mean, 'how come'?"

"I mean a good-looking girl like you . . . "

She put down her hamburger and threw him a withering look. "Are *you* married?"

"No."

"How come? A good-looking guy like you?"

"Oh, let's not get into that again."

"Don't you feel guilty, depriving some poor, frail female of the pleasure of your company and support?"

"I was married once. She wasn't frail. And it was no pleasure. She was doing classified work for NASA, and I'm in the trade. There was hardly a damn thing we could talk about to each other without perpetrating a breach of security."

"Why didn't you find an unclassified job?"

"Why didn't she?"

"Why do you resent her independence?"

"Resent it? I applaud it. She thought it would be demeaning to ask for alimony."

Andrea laughed. "She doesn't sound so bad."

Wade shrugged. "She wasn't."

Andrea sipped her Coke. "You know," she reflected, "my guy and I have the same problem. Hardly anything we can talk about anymore."

"Is he doing classified work?"

"No. He's into oil, and I couldn't care less about strata, viscosity, subterranean reservoirs, gallons per day, dollars per gallon. ! mean, who cares about that? And he feels the same way about what I'm doing."

"Then how did you get together in the first place?"

"A lot of animal itches to scratch, and a little bit of faking took care of the rest of it."

"What happened?"

"The itches are still there, but that's really the only mutual interest we have. It's getting harder and harder to fake the rest."

"Why don't you call it quits?"

"I've thought about it. But there are complications. I'm pregnant."

"Oh!"

"I'm sorry. I didn't mean to shock you."

"Why should it shock me? I guess you'll just have to marry the guy."

"It shocked you." She chewed thoughtfully on her hamburger. "I think marriage would be a mistake. It would be bad for all of us, most of all for the kid."

"What will you do about the kid if you don't marry him?"

"Have it and raise it. It can be done."

"What about your work?"

"Maybe I can do both."

"What about him?"

"Who?"

"The guy you're living with."

Her face went dark. "I don't know."

"The kid will be his kid, too."

"I know." She absentmindedly sucked at the straw, and the last of her Coke gurgled noisily in the bottom of the glass. She put the glass down, opened the pack of cigarettes, and lit one. She puffed at it shallowly a couple of times, not inhaling. "I think we can work something out. He can visit if he wants to. The kid can visit him." She brightened suddenly. "Why not? It'll be the most socially correct part of our entire relationship. It'll be just like we're divorced."

"Why don't you let him raise the kid and you do the monthly visit?"

She considered that for a moment. "I'm not that liberated yet, I don't think."

Wade pushed his chair back from the cart and laughed. "You really are something, you know. I think that kid is going to be okay. You finished?" he asked, indicating the empty plates.

"Looks like."

He put the silver plate covers over the plates and tossed the cigarette pack onto the bed. "I'll just leave this out in the hall for the waiter."

She went to the door and opened it for him, and he rolled the cart out into the hall and set it against the wall.

When he came back in, she closed the door and leaned back against it, the cigarette burning unpuffed between her fingers.

"You know," she said, "I've been thinking."

"About what?"

"Those files."

"All the while you were talking about something else?" he asked.

"That's the way I think best."

"What have you been thinking?"

"I've been thinking that maybe we all owe my father a great big 'thank you' for taking them."

"Maybe," he cautiously agreed.

Chapter
30

Thirty minutes later the phone rang. It was Hull in a high state of agitation.

"Well?" he demanded.

"Well, what?"

"We're waiting. Where the hell is the file?"

"We're waiting, too."

"For what?"

"A communication."

"Are you screwing around with that girl?"

"Trust me."

"Then get off your ass. Sturdivant is about to declare war."

"I thought Sturdivant was the one who called for cooperation."

"He doesn't think we're cooperating. He had this guy Clark in the hospital."

"Does he think we put him in?"

"No. He thinks we spirited him out.

Clark disappeared from his room a little while ago. Now get on the stick." Hull hung up.

At six o'clock they had another cart brought up with chopped sirloin and Coke.

At 6:30 Andrea called the desk to inquire if a special delivery letter had arrived for her. Reply negative.

At seven o'clock the ashtray was full of practically unsmoked butts, and the cigarette pack lay crumpled in the wastebasket. And they were wearing a rut in the carpet with their pacing.

At 7:30 Andrea called the desk again. Still no special delivery letter.

At eight o'clock Andrea struck blood under the cuticle of the index finger on her left hand. She had been gnawing and picking at her nails since seven.

"Dammit," she exclaimed.

"Shall I order some drinks?"

She shook her head and flung herself back on the bed, hand over eyes. "No drinks. The state I'm in, I'm liable to climb the wall on a scotch and soda."

"Why don't you try to catch a nap?"

"How can I nap?" She sat up and perched on her knees on the bed. "I want to scream."

"You want an aspirin?"

"An aspirin?" she asked incredulously. "What kind of sexist are you anyway?"

At nine o'clock Wade got up on an elbow, reached across for the phone, and ordered another cart of food.

"They'll think we're having an orgy up here," he said when he hung up the phone.

"Maybe they'd be right," she replied. She fumbled around the floor for her clothes and began getting dressed.

At 9:30 they were wolfing down hamburgers again when the phone rang. It was Hull. "Well?!"

"We're still waiting," Wade mumbled thickly through a mouthful of ground beef and masticated relish and roll.

"Are you all right?" Hull asked, alarmed.

Wade swallowed hard. "Everything's fine."

"That's better. You sounded like maybe they'd drugged you."

"Who?"

"Maitland and/or Sturdivant. They're both yelling now for an eye for an eye. And they're looking our way."

"Who lost an eye?"

"Nobody. But Maitland's boy Wheeler lost a mouthful of teeth this morning. Had his room and his person ransacked. Whoever hit him must have been wearing brass knuckles."

"Did we do it?"

"No. But Maitland thinks we did, so what's the difference?"

Wade hung up and threw the rest of his hamburger into the wastebasket.

At 10:30 there was a knock at the door. "Special delivery."

It was a big nine-by-four envelope and it was bulging at the seams. When she opened it, she saw why. Charlie Flemming in the post office back home had thoughtfully included a packet of letters on airmail-flimsy recently arrived from Jim. She glanced quickly at the return address on the airmail envelopes to make sure they all were from Jim. Then she tossed them unopened into her purse and turned her attention to the picture postcard. It was an old postcard, its message side yellowing like ancient ivory. Its picture was matte finished and color tinted rather than photographed. It was the kind of postcard that, as a child, she remembered seeing slotted into a display carousel in the Barrows Spa, which was not a spa at all but was the only drugstore on the island. Even then the postcards had had a slightly anachronistic look, like something left over from another era. Mr. Brady, the owner of the Spa, had probably had those cards in a drawer since his boyhood, pictures made before the island had gone into decline, when it had been a resort second only to Newport and Bar Harbor. When Andrea was a little girl, her father used to take her there for a few weeks every summer. She remembered the island as a wondrous place, surrounded by cliff-sheltered beaches. She could wade in the sea or wander along the deserted sand for hours, collecting colored stones polished by the sea, radiant as jewels. Inland there were the "haunted castles," really just the derelict remains of once splendid hotels, but her child's mind had cloaked them in mystery. One by one they had been abandoned, as the island had been abandoned, and one by one they had burned, ignited by vagrant bolts of lightning or by careless campers spending a free night in their shuttered shells. Andrea had delighted in exploring those ruins, unearthing sherds of kitchenware, a dancing slipper, a bit of moldy lace that her imagination could invest with a story.

She studied the faded picture on the postcard: the rock-strewn beach, the chalky cliffs rising behind it, the gabled structure overlooking the sea at the top of the cliff. She remembered it. It was the very beach she had played on. And the wooden building at the top was the hotel in which she had spent those summer weeks of her childhood with her father. There was a long, creaky stairway down the face of the cliff by means of which guests could reach the beach.

Her father, she knew, still spent occasional summers there. The island in its solitude and decline had some special meaning for him which she had never fully understood. It was his cloister, his retreat. When her mother had abandoned them all, he had gone there for a whole month in the winter, and he had come back partially restored.

She saw the "X," freshly drawn in ballpoint ink on the photo just below the hotel, and she knew what it meant. Only she could know. Her father had decided to use the island and the hotel as a haven once again. Crockett's file would be there—probably in the weathered pine cabinet behind the lobby desk marked "Hold for Arrival," waiting for her to claim it.

"Is that it?" Wade's voice startled her. He had been looking over her shoulder as she examined the card, and she had forgotten that he was there.

She looked up. "Yes."

"There's no message."

"Yes, there is."

"That mark he made over the beach?" Wade asked, dismayed. "That's pretty damned vague."

Andrea smiled.

"You think it's amusing? It could take us a week to dig up that much beach."

Andrea was rummaging through her purse.

"Oh!" Wade said hopefully. "You've got an overlay."

"No. A bus schedule." She looked up, puzzled. "At least I thought I had. I picked it up this morning."

"I know you did," Wade said. "You want me to look?"

"What makes you think you can look any better than I can?"

He fixed her with a supercilious expression. "I've been trained."

She held onto the purse. "It doesn't matter. I *know* there's a bus at 11:30. It'll get us to Gunther Point in time to catch the morning ferry."

They got into one of the cabs waiting at the hack stand outside the hotel and asked to be taken to the Port Authority bus terminal. The driver reluctantly folded up his copy of the *Daily News*, switched off the ceiling light, and set his cab in motion.

Wheeler was sitting in the driver's seat of a hearse-black Plymouth parked just behind the hack stand, sipping lukewarm broth from a pulpy cardboard cup. He longed for something solid to eat, but he knew that would be difficult until his gums had healed and a dental bridge could be fitted for the gap where his four front teeth had been. He saw Andrea and Wade get into the cab, watched the cab drive away, dumped what was left of his broth out the window, tossed the crushed remains of his cup under the seat, and followed.

As Wheeler pulled away, a jade-green Mustang made a screeching U-turn from the opposite side of the avenue, barely missing a collision with an oncoming 103 bus. The driver of the Mustang took up his determined pursuit of Wheeler, unaware of how close he had just come to being totaled. His right eye was doggedly focused on the ruby taillights of Wheeler's car. His left eye, the one that should have seen the bus peripherally, was covered by a gauze bandage which was wound round his forehead and encased his cranium like an oversized hockey helmet.

193

He sent two pedestrians scurrying for the relative safety of the sidewalk as he careened around the corner of Fifty-ninth Street, got his bearings, eased up on the accelerator, and fell into formation half a block behind the black Plymouth. His one working eye, bloodshot with the aftereffects of concussion, glowed malevolently. He had been tagging Wheeler since early evening, ever since he'd escaped from the hospital, waiting for that one clear moment when he could wreak vengeance for the insult to his person perpetrated the night before. Nobody beat up Laird Clark and stuffed him in a laundry bin and went unpunished. As he followed the black Plymouth down Seventh Avenue, he was overwhelmed by an impulse to bear down on the gas pedal and close the distance between them and ram, ram, ram. He bit his lip and held himself in check. But he knew the moment was drawing near when he could no longer exercise restraint. He ran his tongue along his lip and tasted blood.

On Eighth Avenue, outside the bus terminal, the cabs were wharfed up three deep, boarding and discharging passengers. A harassed traffic cop, a silver whistle frozen to his teeth, labored valiantly to keep at least a few lanes open to avert a total traffic thrombosis.

Wade and Andrea got out of their cab somewhere in the middle of the avenue and dodged and plunged through the sluggish traffic flow like a pair of broken-field runners.

They made it to the sidewalk and were just about to vanish into the terminal's maw when Wheeler brought his black Plymouth to a lurching halt two lanes away from the curb and leaped out to give chase on foot. He was halfway to the sidewalk and had Andrea and Wade in view when he was brought to a jolting stop by an edifice so formidable and so

194

unyielding that he thought for a moment he had run into one of the ubiquitous taxicabs.

"Where do you think you're headed?" the traffic cop snarled, working the words out around his silver whistle.

"After *them*," Wheeler announced as he pointed toward the building and tried to sidestep around the cop.

The cop, for all his bulk, must have studied with Fred Astaire. He sidestepped right along with Wheeler, maintaining body contact all the way. "Not with your car parked out in the middle of the street, you're not!"

"I'm military intelligence," Wheeler lisped through the gap in his teeth as he watched Andrea and Wade ascending the escalator like a pair of seraphim. He started to reach into his pocket for his ID and then remembered that whoever had mugged him had lifted his wallet.

"And I'm James Bond," growled the cop, neatly following Wheeler's reverse sidestep. "Now get that car out of here before I have it towed away."

The top of the doorway to the terminal was making it increasingly difficult for Wheeler to follow Andrea and Wade's progress on the escalator. It was as if they were rising into the ceiling. He could see them from the hips down, and then the knees down, and then the ankles down, and then they were gone. He turned away from the cop and started back toward his car, did a quick reverse behind a Checker cab and made a run for the sidewalk.

The cop was about to give chase when he was distracted by a green Mustang in the process of being abandoned in the third traffic lane by a creature who looked like a fugitive from a spaceship. The cop planted his feet firmly and waited.

Wheeler took the escalator up to the first level and looked

forlornly about. Andrea and Wade were nowhere in sight. They might be anywhere. The terminal was aswarm with people and as multidecked as an ocean liner. There were half a dozen escalators and elevators and innumerable fire exits and auxiliary stairways. He rode up to the next level, looked around, and realized he could spend the rest of the night in this haphazard kind of search, and intercept them only by chance.

He saw an information booth rising like a lighthouse in the middle of a roiling sea and headed for it.

Tickets in hand, Andrea and Wade came out of the stairway on the third level, looked about, and hurried toward ramp fifteen.

"Wouldn't you know," Andrea panted. "We're at the wrong end of the building. It looks like it's a block away."

"It is a block away."

"And I thought Texas had a monopoly on wide open spaces."

Wade glanced up at one of the clocks on the wall. "No rush. We've got ten minutes."

"Doesn't anybody ever sleep in this town?"

Clots of people restlessly waited with their luggage in front of six of the twenty ramps on the cavernous upper level. Dazed and groggy travelers struggled off newly arrived buses at three other points. An echoing loudspeaker droned incessantly and almost incoherently, announcing arrivals and departures in a disinterested monotone.

There was a change in phrase patterns and in the echoing monotony of the voice on the speaker. Wade stopped and listened. Andrea turned and looked at him quizzically. Wade held up his hand for her to wait. The message was repeated.

"Mr. Hull-l-l waiting-aiting-aiting for associ-ate-ate-ate information booth second-econd-econd level-evel-evel." It
sounded like Bert Lahr doing the cowardly lion.

"What is it?" Andrea asked.

"Hull wants to talk to me." Wade shrugged guiltily. He
knew what she was thinking. "Maybe he got impatient or
suspicious. Maybe he put a backup man on me."

"Maybe you contacted him?"

"How could I have?"

"How should I know? You're the spy."

"I was never out of your sight."

"You people have your ways."

"Oh, Christ! Doesn't anybody trust anybody anymore? I'd
better go down and see what he wants." He glanced at the
clock. "There's time."

"I don't want him along."

"Trust me."

Andrea emitted an exasperated sigh. "You know, dammit, I
do." She watched Wade disappear down the escalator. Then
she turned toward the bus, showed the driver her ticket, and
started to climb aboard.

"Any baggage, ma'am?" he asked. A southern voice,
courtly and kind. She wondered what he was doing on a
route so far from home.

"No baggage."

The driver nodded. "Find a seat, please. We'll be leaving in
eight minutes."

She stepped up into the bus and paused for a moment to
allow her eyes to adjust to the sudden change of light. After
the shadowless neon glare and bouncing echoes of the
terminal, the interior of the bus, with its small, subdued night
lights dotting the overhead, had the ambiance of a movie

theater between shows. Heavy dark upholstery soaking up the sound of muttered conversations; tops of heads, bald, bouffant, varied shades and colors; rustling paper; an infant's sudden spastic cry; a mother's cooing words of comfort; a single sneeze muffled by a handkerchief, and a few tentative coughs. An air of anticipation, as if the big rectangular windshield might be illuminated at any moment by a projected beam and Technicolor images.

The bus was surprisingly full. She had to go halfway up the aisle before she found two vacant seats together. She sat down, folded her hands in her lap, and waited.

Wade found the information booth in the center of the second level and looked about futilely for Hull. He got into line behind two other travelers, intending to ask the girl behind the counter if a message had been left by Mr. Hull.

He felt the blunt pressure of a pistol barrel in the small of his back and heard a voice close to his ear, confidential in tone, professional in manner except for an incongruously childish lisp.

"Would you please step over to that exit sign on the right where we can talk? Walk slowly without turning around. I'll be one step behind you. The weapon in my pocket is a Walther P-38. I don't want to use it, but if forced to, I won't miss. When we've had a chance to talk, I think we can come to an amicable agreement. After all, we're all on the same side, more or less, aren't we?"

When they got over near the exit sign, Wheeler told Wade he could turn around, but warned him against putting his hands in his pockets or making a sudden move.

"Now," Wheeler said, as they faced each other like a couple of old friends, "I had been led to believe that our

198

leaders had come to an agreement whereby we were all to share and share alike. Everything open and aboveboard between us."

"Then why," asked Wade, "did you follow me, and why is your piece aimed at my gut?"

"Why have you run off with the girl without informing our agency that she was moving out?"

"What happened to your teeth?" Wade asked.

"Ask your boss," Wheeler lisped.

"We seem to be answering questions with questions." Wade glanced up at the four-faced clock rotating on a rod suspended from the ceiling over the information booth. It read 11:26.

"I'll ask you one more question," Wheeler said, "and this time I expect an answer. Where were you taking the girl?"

In the dim interior of the bus Andrea glanced anxiously at her watch. It read 11:30. But her watch was probably fast, because 11:30 was departure time, and the bus driver was still standing outside, helping the new arrivals in. She spread her coat across both seats and worked her way to the front of the bus. She stepped down into the bright glare of the terminal and asked the driver how long it would be until they left. He looked at the watch dangling from his belt by a leather fob and told her four minutes.

"I'll be right back," she said, and hurried away.

"We leave right on time, ma'am," he called after her.

She ran toward the nearest escalator and stood at the top, looking down into the second level, but she couldn't see the information booth or Lloyd Wade. The clock on the wall read 11:27. There wasn't time to get to the lower level and find Wade and return before the bus left. It would be foolish to

199

try. Wade might, even now, be on his way up by another stairway, or, if he was still down there, it would be because he was engaging Hull. She hurried back to ramp fifteen and waited near the departure gate within a few steps of the bus. If Wade didn't show, he had at least succeeded partly in his purpose in traveling with her. He had guaranteed her freedom of movement. The clock on the wall read 11:29.

Wade watched the big second hand on the clock above the information booth move inexorably toward departure time. He was wondering if Wheeler would really shoot if he ran. He didn't think he would shoot. But he would follow. If Wade ran, he would lead Wheeler straight to Andrea.

A character kept drifting in and out of Wade's field of vision, looking like a fugitive from a monster movie with his head encased in a lopsided mushroom of gauze. Clark kept moving closer and closer, maneuvering through the crowd furtively, like a stalking cat, until he stood less than five yards abeam of Wheeler's right ear.

To Wade's disbelieving eyes it appeared he was prepared to spring.

"I think," Wade said almost casually to Wheeler, "that we're about to be jumped by a looney."

Wheeler just had time to say, "What kind of answer is that to my question?" when the figure came catapulting through the air, trailing streamers of gauze and growling gutturally.

Wheeler stumbled sideways, locked in the rib-crushing embrace of the flying figure. His index finger tensed involuntarily around the trigger of the pistol in his pocket. The Walther went off with a bang, the reverberations of which sounded like a fusillade in the echoing hall. The crowd scattered like a flock of pigeons frightened by backfire.

200

Wheeler felt his toes go numb and realized, to his dismay, that he must have shot himself in the foot.

They went down like dominoes: Clark on top of Wheeler, Wheeler on top of Wade. Wade tried to crawl out from under the pileup, but Wheeler managed to worm a hand free and clamped it like a bear trap around Wade's ankle. Wade labored heroically to free himself, dragging the weight of two men behind him, inch by inch across the smooth marbled floor. Clark sat astride Wheeler's back, like some demented broncobuster, his legs locked around Wheeler's rib cage, pummeling Wheeler about the head and ears, yelling, "Nobody clobbers Laird Clark and dumps him in a laundry basket."

Suddenly Wade was free. He scrambled to his feet and bolted for the fire stairs. He glanced back once as he shoved open the door and saw two uniformed guards pulling Wheeler and Clark apart and hauling them to their feet. One of the guards shouted at Wade, "Hey, you! Wait!" But Wade went into the stairwell, letting the door slam on the chaos behind him, and the guard had his hands too full of Clark to follow.

Clark and Wheeler were facing the wall, feet spreadeagled, arms out, palms flat against the surface.

"Who fired the shot?" one of the guards wanted to know as the frisk began.

"He did!" Clark yelled.

"He jumped me first," Wheeler protested.

"What kind of excuse is that?" the guard demanded, fishing the Walther out of Wheeler's pocket.

"I've got a permit," Wheeler announced a bit stridently.

"To go shooting in a crowded hall?" the guard asked.

"Nobody got shot but me, so what's the fuss? It was an accident."

"Reckless endangerment is what it was, and you're under arrest."

"Again?!" Wheeler sighed and stared down at his blood-stained shoe.

Wade leaped up the fire stairs, two at a time, to the third level and found himself confronted by a locked steel door with a sheet metal sign riveted to its face. "Fire Exit Only. No Entrance."

He turned around and took the stairs down, finding the doors locked from the stairwell side at every level except the bottom. He shoved that door open, went through, and found himself standing on the sidewalk outside the terminal building on Forty-first Street.

He ran down Forty-first Street to Eighth Avenue and elbowed his way through the perpetually milling crowds outside the main entrance to the terminal. He got a foothold on the moving stairway and began the tortoise-paced upward ride. He wished he could run, but his way was blocked by the jelled mass of travelers ahead of him. Halfway to the first level he saw Wheeler and his assailant on the descending escalator, bracketed by uniformed guards, eyes downcast, hands clasped in front of them, solemn as figures at a urinal.

Wade began looking for an escape route in case Wheeler looked up and saw him. The only way off was over the side, but since he was more than halfway to the first level, he'd probably be lucky if he broke no more than an ankle when he landed. Wheeler looked up and saw him. Wade braced himself to jump. Wheeler raised his shackled wrists shoulder

202

high, clasping his hands in a gladiatorial salute, and carefully mouthed the words, "Good luck!" Wheeler seemed almost relieved.

Wade continued his tortuous ascent. When he finally arrived at the top level, it was 11:38 by the clock on the wall. He sprinted down the length of the great hall to ramp fifteen, his hopes rising as he saw the clot of travelers shifting restlessly near the loading platform. But the travelers were waiting for the next bus due in, the "OVERNIGHT SPECIAL TO CINCINNATI," according to the new sign that had been affixed to the callboard. Wade's bus to New England had gone and Andrea had gone with it.

Chapter

31

The bus lumbered down the exhaust-blackened, spiraling ramps, diesel whining, air brakes hissing, like a creature in distress, until finally it settled into its element on the roomy horizontal blacktop of Tenth Avenue. Traffic was thin on Tenth Avenue, and the driver began an easy twenty-five-mile-an-hour northward roll, the timed lights turning green as he approached each corner, as if an invisible switchman were changing them especially for him.

The seat beside Andrea was empty. She stared out the window at the dismal tenements, the garish corner hamburger joints, the junkies and the drunks nodding in the doorways. She wished that Wade were with her. She felt very much alone. She thought she'd like to call him when she got back; there was a feeling of incompleteness about it all. She wondered, if she called his "seminary," if he'd still be there. She wondered if the number would still be a working exchange by tomorrow.

The bus crossed the garish intersection at Seventy-second Street and Broadway and rolled up Amsterdam Avenue, deep into the upper West Side of Manhattan, past urban redevelopment sites gouged by acres of craters and watched over by mammoth locustlike cranes. It looked like the aftermath of a disaster, or the forerunner of one. Blitzkrieg—by real estate speculator or by bomber—the effect was the same. Past the sleeping campus of Columbia University, through the restless streets of Harlem, into the most northern tip of the island, then east through a thunderous slot called the Cross Bronx Expressway.

Wade grabbed a bus schedule and took the fire stairs. Outside, on Forty-first Street, he got his bearings and began to run toward Ninth Avenue. The area west of Ninth was honeycombed with park-and-lock lots earning a few easy bucks while waiting to be converted into clusters of boxy glass towers that would mirror one another with numbing monotony.

At the corner of Ninth Avenue he stopped and looked south and then north and saw, a couple of blocks away near Forty-third Street, a big plywood sign painted in orange and white Day-Glo, PARK, and the gaping flattened area like a missing tooth that indicated an open lot.

He walked as quickly as he could, but walked, lest he look like a fleeing purse snatcher to a cruising police car. A lunatic image popped into his head: a family of tourists arriving with picnic baskets at one of the ubiquitous areas labeled "Park."

The parking lot, which covered the entire block from Ninth to Tenth Avenue, was surrounded by a temporary hurricane fence and was attended disinterestedly by a man in a booth on the Ninth Avenue side.

Wade waved at the man in the booth as if he belonged there and strolled casually toward the far side of the lot. There were maybe fifty cars scattered around an area that in midday would hold a couple of hundred. He headed toward a cluster of four or five cars near the Tenth Avenue side of the lot, brushing close to the cars that happened to be in his path, nonchalantly trying the door handles as he passed. He didn't think he'd find an easy opener. People were too damn thief-conscious these days. As he walked, he worked his belt loose from around his waist, drew it out of the loops in his trousers, rolled it up, and tucked it into his pocket. Wade charted his course into an area where the positioning of the cars would screen him from the attendant's view, if the attendant was watching at all, which Wade doubted. When he got to the far corner of the lot, he took his key ring out of his pocket, selected the biggest key on the ring and approached one of the cars in the cluster of five, a Pontiac of reasonably recent vintage which looked as if it had been well maintained.

He worked his key in between the top of the window and the weatherseal. Using the key as a lever and the minimal play in the roller gears to his advantage, he managed to force the window down about half an inch. That was as far as it would go, but it was far enough.

He took his belt from his pocket and carefully let it down, buckle first, through the half-inch gap in the window. He played out the belt until the buckle settled on the sill of the window, between the glass and the safety lock, which was set in the top of the door like a golf tee. He let the belt out another notch and the buckle flopped down over the head of the safety lock.

He reeled the belt in slowly. As the buckle rose, it pulled the safety lock up with it.

He tried the door and it opened. He quickly tucked himself into the car, closed the door, reached in under the dashboard, and ripped out the thin composition-board shield that protected the ignition wiring. He poked around in the spaghettilike maze, found the two leads he wanted, yanked them out of their fittings, and touched the uninsulated ends together. There was a blue-white flash, followed by the thunderclap of the big V-8 turning over. He twisted the wire ends together and eased his foot down on the accelerator. The engine ran smoothly. He checked the needle on the gas gauge. Three-quarters full. He'd picked a winner. He let the engine idle, flicked on the overhead light, searched among the road maps in the pouch in the door, and found one for New England. He opened up his bus schedule and laid it flat on the dashboard shelf. He unfolded the map and checked it against the few stops the bus made between New York and Portland and determined from these points of reference the route that the bus would most likely take to Gunther Point. He put the map down on the seat beside him and turned off the overhead light. Then he flicked on his headlights and released the parking brakes. He glanced at his watch. It was 11:45. The bus had a fifteen-minute lead on him. Exercising restraint, he rolled toward the exit on Ninth Avenue at a respectable fifteen miles an hour. As his headlights played on the Plexiglas window of the booth, the attendant glanced up, laid his newspaper down, and busied himself with something on his desk. Wade applied a little more pressure to the accelerator—and wished he hadn't. The attendant leaped out of the booth, right into the path of the oncoming car, and held up his hands for Wade to stop. Wade had two options. He could run right over the man or he could stop. He brought the car pitching to a halt and barely missed running over the man anyway. The attendant, unruffled, reached across the hood of the car and plucked a small buff-colored card from under the windshield wiper. He examined the card and then leaned in at the window.

"That'll be four dollars and seventy-five cents."

"Four seventy-five?" Wade repeated, puzzled.

"For three hours and forty-five minutes. It's right up there on the sign." He pointed to the rate card tacked to the side of the booth.

Wade let out a low whistle. The attendant thought it was a whistle of protest over the high cost of parking. It was relief. He handed the man a five-dollar bill.

The man took it and started toward the booth for change.

"Keep it," Wade yelled gratefully. He rolled out into Ninth Avenue, turned west, picked up the elevated Miller Highway at Forty-second Street, sped north along the inky Hudson River, past the yacht basin at Seventy-ninth Street with its hibernating houseboats, the skyscraper bell tower of Riverside Church near 120th Street, the massive new blocks of apartment buildings on the Jersey side, crowding the river, dwarfing the Palisades. At 175th Street, under the legs of the George Washington Bridge, he veered right and took the feeder road into the Cross Bronx Expressway. He bore down on the accelerator, heading east toward the Bruckner interchange and the entrance to U.S. 95, the New England Throughway, the fast superhighway the bus would be traveling on its express journey to Boston. There was a clear straight stretch ahead, and he decided to test the car's handling and performance. He ground the accelerator down into the floorboard and got the car up to a little over eighty miles an hour, but the suspension wasn't up to the engine's capabilities. The bouncing and buffeting was almost uncontrollable. He went over an asphalt seam in the roadway and bottomed out and hoped he hadn't torn his gas tank off. He eased up on the gas pedal and found that the car was controllable and behaved well enough at seventy-five. He figured the bus would be doing seventy pretty steadily all the way. The bus was scheduled to arrive in Boston at about four in the morning. He figured he should have the bus in sight sometime between two and three o'clock. Then he'd decide what to do. If his tires held out, and his gas supply.

His headlights picked up the ganglionic confusion of the Bruckner interchange, feeder roads branching and dividing, offering a dizzying array of alternatives. He scanned the green and white signs, iridescent in the headlight beams. "Bronx River Parkway Bear Left"; "Throgs Neck Bridge" and an arrow left; "Whitestone Bridge," arrow right; "New England Throughway." He sped in under the road-spanning sign and headed north.

The bus was passing Stamford, fifty-five minutes out of New York, each of its passengers cocooned in his own private world. Some had settled into sleep. Others were still turning and rustling the pages of the newspapers and magazines they had purchased before departure. A woman across the aisle from Andrea was bent over a hand mirror which she had braced between her knees and was pinning up her hair.

Andrea looked down at the thin packet of letters in her

hand, the letters from Jim that had been forwarded along with her father's postcard. She had already read two of them. The third one would merely be a repetition of the second, which had been a repetition of the first, which had been a reflection of the most recent months of their relationship. Mechanical declarations of love, mixed with truly heartfelt descriptions of bore samplings, sulfur content, potential production of barrels per day converted into production of dollars per year percentaged out to personal income share, converted into rooms per house, children per room, cars per garage, memberships per country club. And, she had mentally interjected, the inevitable and increasing number of Bloody Marys per day to blot out the monotony of it all.

With bemused awareness she realized that through all the trauma and terror of the past few days, she hadn't once wished that Jim were with her; she hadn't even thought about him until the letters had arrived. It was over. There would be a scene when she got home; there would be no way of avoiding it, not unless she just packed her things and stole away in the night, and she wasn't the type to do that. There would be a scene because she would have voided the blueprint that Jim had drawn up for his life . . . and hers. Well, she would just have to face it. She tore the packet of airmail-flimsy in half and glanced right and left, looking for a litter bag.

And saw her brother's face reflected in the hand mirror of the woman across the aisle. The woman had raised the mirror in order to examine her eyebrows, and the angle had been just right, for just a moment, but that moment was enough. Lenny was in an aisle seat a few rows behind her. And the fact that he seemed to be thoroughly engrossed in the comic book he was reading didn't in the least diminish the clammy feeling of terror that all but overwhelmed Andrea.

210

Chapter

32

Wade tapped his horn and pulled out into the center lane, pushed his accelerator to the floor, and, bucketing and swaying, began crawling at close to eighty miles an hour past the mammoth tractor trailer on his right. For a moment the roar was deafening as he hovered abreast of the big truck's cab and engine, fighting to control the wheel, watching his speedometer needle crawl up between eighty and eighty-five miles an hour. The damned truck driver was trying to make a race of it, probably to relieve the boredom of an overnight run. He hazarded a glance up at the cab of the truck and saw the driver grinning down at him, his face eerie in the greenish glow of the instrument panel.

Finally, the trucker waved and eased back on his throttle and Wade shot ahead, anxiously putting some distance between them before slowing at last to seventy-five and pulling back into the right-hand lane. He wiped the sweat away from his eyes and saw the sign flash by. "Stamford, 5 mi." He glanced at the clock on the dashboard. He had been traveling for a little under fifty minutes. The bus was somewhere up ahead of him, some fifteen miles ahead, and it would be somewhere in the neighborhood of two hours before he had its taillights in sight.

Abeam of the bus and to the west, the neo-Gothic profile of Yale University stood out in distant silhouette against the moonlit transparency of the night sky. The towers inched backward and finally disappeared from view as the bus bore northward past New Haven.

Aside from the rumble of the engine, it was dead quiet inside the bus. The newspapers and magazines had been tucked away. The infants aboard had settled into sleep, and most of the adults had, too. The pinpoint reading lights had been switched off. Those passengers who were still awake sat staring into the darkness or at occasional lighted road signs.

Andrea wasn't sleeping. Her initial panic had abated, but her mind was racing. She remembered the bus schedule that had been in her purse. He must have taken it out when he had her trapped in the elevator. She had checked off the departure times. He must have been waiting as each of those buses loaded up. He may have already been on the bus when she had arrived at ramp fifteen. He may have gotten aboard while she was searching for Wade. She wondered why, with Wade gone, he hadn't moved in next to her. She decided that he didn't want her to know he was there. He planned to lay back, keep hands off, maintain his distance, and let her unwittingly lead him to Crockett's file. Threatening as his presence was, she felt she had an advantage as long as she knew he was there and he didn't know that she knew.

Andrea decided that when they got to Boston, she would check into a hotel rather than make the connection to the morning ferry to Barrows Island as she had earlier planned to do. She would phone Wade in New York and wait until he joined her. She didn't want to make the trip to the island alone with her brother in pursuit. Until Wade arrived she could hole up in her room, or, safer still, get onto one of the guided tours that trucked tourists around the city's parks and monuments for a morning or an afternoon.

A road sign flashed past. "Guilford, 5 mi." And then another sign. "Construction ahead. Detour Guilford. U.S. 1A."

Wade came into reading range of the detour sign twelve minutes later. He knew that the bus would have had to take the detour, too. Twenty minutes at the most, he figured, until he'd have the bus in sight.

He swung onto 1A, accelerated up to seventy-five and then judiciously eased off by about ten miles an hour. The headlights of an oncoming vehicle momentarily blinded him, leaving black spots dancing on his retinas. After the arrow-straight, island-divided turnpike this was going to be hell. One-A was a three-lane blacktop, badly pitted and sharply curving. One lane of traffic each way, with the middle lane for passing. He couldn't do better than sixty-five without risking killing himself. But then the bus would have to throttle back, too.

The car shimmied in the backwash of a passing tractor trailer. He hung on to the wheel for dear life.

As the bus passed the Niantic interchange, the driver slowed a little and intoned in a voice keyed to the drone of the engine that they were approaching a gas stop equipped with washrooms and sandwich and soft drink dispensers. Anyone who wished to avail himself of the facilities would have ten minutes time in which to do so. There would be no additional stops before Boston.

Lenny Blue, dozing two rows behind his sister, blinked himself awake and looked about, confused and disoriented. He was almost certain he had heard the word "Boston" come drifting through gauzy layers of unconsciousness. He had allowed himself to drop off, secure in the knowledge that Andrea couldn't leave the bus before Boston, and Boston was hours away. He peered through sleep-swollen eyes at the wooded countryside flashing by, certainly no metropolitan suburb. He brought his wristwatch up close to his eyes and read 2:20. They weren't due in Boston until sometime around four. He must have dreamed the word. He pressed the watch to his ear to make sure it was still ticking. Then, satisfied, he let his hand drop and his heavy eyelids close.

Ten minutes later the driver took his foot off the gas pedal and held it poised over the brake. The bus glided toward the exit lane marked "Rest Stop." Two rows of pumps were lined up about thirty yards in front of a one-story glass-faced canteen which housed an array of automatic vending machines. The driver tapped his brakes lightly a couple of times to promote deceleration. By the time the bus drew abreast of the gas pumps a little gentle toe pressure was all that was needed to bring the fifteen-ton vehicle to an almost imperceptible halt.

Wade's headlights picked up the sign. "Rest Stop 12 mi. Open 24 Hours." His legs were stiff, his hands were cramped from hanging onto the wheel, his eyes felt like they were going to pop right out of their sockets.

A cup of black coffee and a few deep knee bends might make all the difference in the world. But it would also delay him at least five minutes, a five-minute gap that might take another hour to close. It wasn't so much the extra hour that worried him; it was what might happen during that hour. He might blow a tire, his radiator might go, his engine might fail. The more time that separated him from the bus, the greater was the chance of a malfunction that could strand him until morning.

On the other hand, if he didn't stop and rest, some personal malfunction, some lapse of concentration or of coordination might wipe him out forever.

Ten or twelve stiff, groggy passengers shuffled somnambulistically down the aisle of the bus and stepped creakily onto the gravel walk. They fanned slowly out across the open area in front of the canteen: men's room to the left, ladies' room to the right, vending machines behind the big glass window in the center. Everything was coin-operated. There wasn't an attendant in sight. Andrea imagined that there would be people in during the day to stock the machines and pump gas. But at this hour the facility was abandoned. The driver got out of the bus, unlocked one of the pumps with a key, and began filling his tank with diesel fuel.

A few more passengers got up. Andrea began to worry. If the bus emptied, she would be left alone with Lenny. Even if he made no overt move, it would be difficult for her to sustain the pretense that he wasn't there. She wondered if it might not be safer and more natural for her to go up to the canteen along with the others.

A couple of people were standing in the aisle between her row of seats and Lenny's. Andrea slowly got to her feet, pretended to yawn, stretched, and, taking advantage of the screen that the people in the aisle afforded, casually glanced toward the back of the bus, keeping her eyes moving to minimize the chance of making contact with her brother.

She noted, to her great relief, that the bus was still at least half-full. Those passengers who hadn't gotten up seemed to be dozing. Lenny's chin was down on his chest. She wondered if he was still reading his comic book. She pretended to yawn again and hazarded another look. He wasn't reading. He was asleep.

Her heart racing, Andrea slipped out into the aisle. If there was a phone in the canteen, she could call Lloyd and let him know what had happened.

She stepped off the bus onto the gravel walk, feeling like a space traveler returning to earth after a long and hazardous voyage into limbo.

As she hurried up the shallow slope to the canteen, it occurred to her that she needn't return to the bus at all. If Lenny slept for just a little while longer, the bus would leave and he would be well on his way to Boston before he realized she was gone.

She heard footsteps on the gravel behind her. She tensed, fought back an impulse to run, waited for the crushing grip of his hand on her shoulder.

A man and a woman hurried past her, breaths condensing, intent on reaching the warmth and shelter of the canteen. Andrea shuddered. She forced herself to look back. If he was watching, she would have to follow the others into the canteen as if nothing had happened, get a cup of coffee, and do her best to drink it. Then she would have no choice but to return to the bus when the others did and continue the journey to Boston, and pray that he didn't realize that she had seen him.

He hadn't left the bus. She scanned the windows and saw him, in dim profile, still slumped in his seat on the far side of the aisle.

She hurried on toward the canteen. The bright, glass-fronted room would afford her poor cover. When the other passengers returned to the bus, she would stand out in there like a figure on a well-lighted stage. There was a ladies' toilet to the right of the canteen. She could wait in there, lock herself into a stall until the bus left.

She hesitated for a moment. As she was about to take the path to the right, she saw a rectangular blue sign affixed to the canteen's interior back wall: PUBLIC TELEPHONE. She decided to try to get her call through to Lloyd immediately, before the canteen began to empty. She pushed through the door, past knots of people gnawing at their sandwiches and gulping their coffee. There was a change machine on the wall. She slipped the machine two one-dollar bills and got a handful of assorted coins. She looked back through the window at the bus. Lenny hadn't moved.

She dialed the number of the "seminary" in New York, and wasn't surprised at all when an alert switchboard girl picked up almost immediately. Seminaries of this special type, she had learned, never slept.

"Mr. Wade, please," Andrea asked. "It's urgent."

"Reverend Wade is unavailable at the moment," the switchboard girl replied.

"It's a case of extreme emergency," Andrea persisted.

"Who is calling?" the operator asked.

"Tell him Andrea Tobin."

"Ah, Miss Tobin. One moment, please."

There was a pause followed by the clicking sounds of circuits being switched. The line seemed to go dead for a moment. Then she heard a man's voice, high-pitched, scratchy, and thick-tongued with sleep. The board girl must have just wakened him. But whoever she had wakened, it wasn't Wade.

"What do you mean, where can you reach him, Miss Tobin? He's supposed to be with you."

"Who is this?" Andrea asked.

"Hull."

She remembered that Hull was Wade's boss. "We got separated in New York."

"In New York?" He exploded. "You mean you've *left* New York?"

"Yes."

"And he's not with you?"

"No."

"Well, where the hell is he?"

"I thought your office would know; that's why I called."

"And where the hell are you?"

She hesitated. "That's none of your business, Mr. Hull."

"Not my business? Little lady, you've got . . . "

"An agreement," she cut him off.

"A what?"

"We agreed, remember; Lloyd was to stay with me, no one else."

"Then why the hell didn't he?"

"You paged him."

"I what?"

"Paged him. At the bus terminal. That's how we got separated."

"Oh Christ!"

"You mean you didn't?" she asked weakly.

"I didn't even know you were at any bus terminal. Now where are you?"

"What about Lloyd?" she asked, alarmed.

"I'll put a trace on him. We'll find him if he's still in one piece. If he's not, we'll find the pieces. Do you have the files with you?"

"Oh, God!"

"I said, do you have the files with you?"

"No."

"Where are they?"

She hesitated.

"Let's quit playing games, little lady. You see where games have gotten us."

She didn't answer. She was thinking of Wade, maybe dead somewhere. She could see her brother's profile in the seat in the bus. She swallowed. Her lips tasted salty. Her cheeks were wet. There was the flavor of tears on her tongue. Games? She wasn't having any fun.

"Where are they?" Hull persisted. She didn't answer. She looked over toward where the bus was parked. Some of the passengers were starting to straggle aboard. She could still see Lenny's silhouette. A few minutes more and the bus would be gone. Just a few minutes more.

"Where are you calling from, Miss Tobin?"

She hung up.

A couple left the room and hurried across the walk to join the others on the bus. If she waited much longer, she would be highly visible in the wide open room. She left the canteen and took the path around to the side of the building. As she opened the door to the toilet, she took one last look back at the bus, but the aisle was now filled with people, and her view of the seats on the far side was obscured. A woman brushed past her, hurrying from the toilet. "Better shake a leg, hon," she sang out in passing.

The toilet was empty. Cold tile and green soap smell. Andrea locked herself into one of the stalls and sat down; she was exhausted. She looked at her watch. The bus would be leaving in two or three minutes. She closed her eyes and waited.

When she heard the starting rumble of the big diesel engine, she unlocked the stall and went to the outside door. She pushed the door open a crack and peered out. The bus was locked up tight. The driver turned on his headbeams. Slowly, like a mammoth waking itself from a long slumber, the bus began to roll, its six big tires crunching hungrily on the graveled roadway.

A big tractor trailer came thundering past on the highway, heading south. Andrea pushed the door open wider and stood with her back against it, watching as the bus picked up speed on the exit track and wobbled into the highway's northbound lane, and finally disappeared around a curve behind a screen of trees.

She stood there for a moment, leaning against the open door, unmindful of the penetrating cold, limp with relief, overwhelmed by the sudden stillness that had descended on the place. The forecourt was eerily lighted by the neon overspill through the window of the canteen. A sandwich wrapper dropped by a careless passenger twisted and leaped spasmodically around the walkway. Otherwise there was no movement. There was no sound either, except for the hissing of the wind.

A pale wash of headlights appeared in the northbound lane and began to creep like a slow phosphorescent tide northward along the highway. She ran out of the shelter of the doorway toward the highway, hopeful of flagging down the approaching vehicle. She took no more than five steps and stopped, brought up short by the sound of a door slamming shut behind her. She whirled, looked back, exhaled a plume of steamy breath, and relaxed. It was the door to the ladies' toilet. The wind had swung it shut. She started to turn back toward the highway, and froze. Something had moved across the line of trees behind the building. The tall figure of a man.

Lloyd Wade picked up the sign in his headlights. "Rest Stop 1000 Feet" and an arrow pointing right. The invitation was almost irresistible. He desperately needed that five-minute break. Even if it put him another hour's traveling time behind the bus, it would be worth it. He was about to lift his foot off the gas pedal and let the car lose momentum when he saw taillights disappearing around a curve about half a mile ahead. Four taillights, two of them much too high to belong to a car. A truck? Maybe. Or maybe it was the bus he was chasing. Peripherally he saw the approach lane to the rest stop flash past as he bore down on the accelerator.

Andrea turned again, in time to see the car flash past heading north, and then the highway was again engulfed in darkness. She whirled back to face the squat building. Squinting against the glare of the light from the canteen, she tried to see into the darkness behind the building.

He waited until the car had passed, and then separated himself from the dark mass of concrete and foliage. He was just a few feet behind where she had stood in the shelter of the open door. He must have been standing there behind her all the time, as she had watched the bus drive away. Her stomach turned over. He took a few steps sideways, vanishing and materializing and vanishing again, dark and sleek: a taunting apparition alternately melding with and becoming separate from the silhouettes of the trees.

She began to back away toward the highway, though she knew that the odds were against another car coming by.

"Andrea!" His voice cracked out like a rifle shot. She stopped and watched, mesmerized, as he moved out into the light in the front of the building.

Then, the spell of shape and shadow and flickering image broken, she turned and ran. She heard heavy footsteps pounding behind her, slamming hard against the ground, crunching gravel.

Ahead of her on the highway there was no light, no sign at all that a vehicle might be coming. She looked backward as she ran and saw him closing on her. She gasped, jolted by the pain of a tearing tendon as her foot rolled over a stone. She felt herself pitching forward onto the sharp gravel. And then his hand was clamped around her wrist. She screamed. Just once.

"Scream your damn head off," he snarled. "See what good it does you." He hauled her up by the wrist, her shoulder separating and snapping back into place.

He yanked her toward the building. She fell and cried out, "My ankle."

He jerked her to her knees, then shifted his hold. Encircling her upper arm in a bruising grip, he hauled her upright again. She stood, shuddering, her weight on her left foot.

"Move!" he ordered.

Supporting her weight with his hand, he propelled her, painfully limping, toward the canteen.

Wade had closed the distance between himself and the lead vehicle to less than a quarter of a mile. His headlights, at the end of their range, faintly delineated the area around the four red taillights: the high rear profile, the wide rear window. It was the bus. Elated, he felt he could follow the monster at this range all the way to Boston. But his judgment warned him that that would be a mistake. He had been battling exhaustion only a few minutes ago. It was bound to catch up with him sooner or later, perhaps with fatal results on the highway, certainly with a loss of alertness when he might need it most on the last leg of their journey to Barrows Island.

He bore down on the accelerator. Fifty yards. He dipped and raised his headlights, signaling his intention to pass. Twenty-five yards. He started to pull out, was pinioned by the oncoming beams of a tractor trailer, tucked himself in behind the bus again and then realized that he had the middle lane for passing. He *had* lost his well-honed edge of awareness. He pulled out again, hanging onto the wheel as he fought the buffeting from the wash of the passing truck. He crawled even with the bus, even with the driver's window. The bus slowed a little to let him draw head and into the right-hand lane.

He pulled ahead and drifted to the right. At seventy-five miles an hour he straddled the line between the right and center lanes, pulling about fifty yards ahead of the bus. Then, rolling down his window, he held his hand out, upraised, and began to slow down.

The bus driver tooted his horn impatiently, signaling Wade to move to the right.

Wade held his position on the line so that the bus couldn't pass, and continued to decelerate. He flipped on his rear blinkers as a further warning. They were down to forty-five miles an hour now. The bus driver pounded his horn. Wade slowed some more.

The bus driver, at the end of his patience, swung out beyond the middle lane toward the southbound lane in an attempt to pass. Wade drifted over with him. The bus moved right. Wade moved right. They drifted left and right along the road like jinking aircraft, but they were losing speed all the while. Wade had slowed down to twenty-five miles an hour. He hoped the bus driver was alert and that he had enough stopping room. He thrust his hand out in the stop signal again and gingerly depressed his brake pedal. There was an explosive hiss of air cylinders behind him as the bus driver fought his vehicle to a stop, practically overriding the top of Wade's car.

Wade and the bus driver hit the pavement at the same instant. The driver had his fists clenched; his face was livid. Wade held his hand up placatingly.

Lenny propelled Andrea ahead of him into the canteen and let go with a shove. Her weight came down on the bad ankle and it gave way. She went down on a knee and elbow and slid half a yard across the tile floor. She started to get up, and he kicked the good leg out from under her. She went down again on her hands and knee. "Stay where you are." He went to the wall, turned off the big ceiling lights. The only illumination in the room spilled out from the little square windows of the sandwich machines.

He towered over her, legs set wide apart, breathing hard. He waited a moment, trying to bring himself under control, restraining an overpowering urge to break her into little pieces, knowing that if he did, if he allowed himself to give vent to his rage over twenty-nine years of bitterness and frustration, he would wind up empty-handed again. When he finally spoke, his tone was almost conciliatory.

"Now, listen to what I'm saying, Andrea." She stared down at the floor and shook her head. "And look at me when I'm talking to you." He placed the tip of his shoe carefully under her chin and raised it, really quite gently, until her eyes were looking up into his, ablaze with anger. She shoved his foot out of the way with the flat of her hand. He let it pass.

He warned her, "You know I can hurt you. You remember how I can hurt you? Only I really don't want to hurt you anymore. Tell me where the old man put those files and that'll be the end of it."

She didn't say a word. She glared at him defiantly.

He shrugged, went to the telephones, and ripped the receivers out, cords and all. He took out his knife and cut the receivers off the cords. Then he put his knife away.

He looped one of the cords around her wrists. "You know, I don't do a lot of things real good, but I'm really good at this." He tied a knot in the cord. "I suppose people are really good at what they really get a kick out of doing." He looped the other cord around her ankle and pulled tight. She winced. "Sorry," he said. "I didn't mean to hurt you, yet. You can still save yourself a lot of pain." He waited a moment but got no response. "No?" He shrugged. "Okay."

He took hold of the cord around her ankles and stood up, tipping her onto her back. She sucked in air, gasping with pain, as he dragged her by her ankles across the tile floor.

She was breathing hard through clenched teeth, but she didn't cry out as he swung her around in front of the coffee vendor, hauled her into a sitting position, and propped her against the machine just below the little plastic window where the cups were filled.

Then he stood up again, embraced the adjacent sandwich machine, and dragged it away from the wall. He squeezed in behind the machine and began humming cheerfully, if slightly off-key. He interrupted his rendition of "Camptown Races" to mutter to no one in particular, "Oh, yeah! This is going to work out nice."

He pulled the plug out of the wall socket, took out his knife, and cut off the cable where it went into the back of the machine. He came out from behind the machine, trailing the cable and the plug.

He cut around the cable with his knife, about an inch from the end where it had fed into the machine, and began stripping off the insulation. He had the copper wire neatly exposed in less than a minute. He stood a moment to admire his work. "One of the trades they taught me in the slammer. Electrical wiring. They said it would come in handy someday."

He squeezed in behind the machine and stuck the plug into the wall socket, then came out, carrying the lead end of the wire by the insulated section, being very careful not to touch the live inch of copper at the tip.

He knelt just behind her in the space between the machines and talked softly into her ear. "Remember," he asked, "when we were kids and I unscrewed the light bulb in

226

the lamp on the living room table and I dropped a penny into the socket and I told you you could keep it if you could take it out?"

She remembered. Her finger probing for the penny, the paralyzing jolt and the current vibrating through her, and she unable to let go. Standing there screaming until her father pulled her away. And her brother laughing until his laughter was stopped by a paternal smack across the face. She had never fully overcome an irrational fear of things electrical.

And now her brother was whispering into her ear and holding the bright copper end of the wire out for her to see. "Remember how it felt?"

He touched the copper lead to her earlobe, ever so lightly and fleetingly. Her body arched in a brief, terrifying spasm. Then she crumpled in on herself, panting, fighting to keep from crying out.

"That was just a sample," Lenny said softly. "Think what it would be like if I held it there for a second, for two seconds. Think about it, because that's what I'm going to do. The first time you don't answer my questions I'll give you about a half-second jolt; that's about twice what I just gave you. And that'll just be starters. Sooner or later you'll tell me what I want to know. The sooner the better for both of us. Okay?

"Now, where did the old man put that file?"

She was staring down at her knees, bracing herself for the jolt, trying to keep her body from trembling and betraying how scared she was. The room suddenly went bright, like a sunburst, as if all the lights had been turned on at once. She brought her head up and found herself squinting into the headlights of an oncoming car. It was speeding straight at the canteen, right across the lawn and gravel walk. It lurched to a stop directly in front of the big window. The driver's door flew open. A figure was running toward the entrance to the canteen.

"Lloyd!" she cried out, and then opened her mouth again to shout a warning, and found herself gagging. Lenny had shoved a balled handkerchief into her mouth, between her tongue and her palate. With her hands bound by the telephone cords, there was no way she could remove it. She twisted her head to look at where Lenny had been squatting behind her shoulder, but he was gone, back somewhere behind the vending machine.

She turned again and saw Wade coming through the doorway, running toward her. She tried to shout again, and began to choke.

Wade was kneeling beside her, probing her mouth for the gag, and she wasn't helping, shaking her head violently from side to side, trying to warn him.

The handkerchief came trailing out, and behind it her shouted alarm.

"My brother!"

Wade looked up and tried to throw himself to the side, too late. The looped cable dropped down over his head. Lenny had unplugged it from the wall and was using it as a garrote.

Wade was down on his back, thrashing, helpless, as Lenny knelt over him pulling the loop tighter.

"Now, Sister!" His voice had lost its calm and reasoning tone. It was raspy and harsh and slightly out of control as he struggled to hold Wade down. "No more games. You've got about two minutes to tell me what I want to know. That's how long it'll take your friend here to die. After that I'll start on you again."

Wade was hardly moving now. His neck had swelled above the loop; his face was turning a deep magenta.

Andrea heard herself yelling. "The Sea Cliff Hotel."

"The what?" Lenny demanded.

Wade was thumping his heel weakly against the floor.

"The Sea Cliff Hotel!" she shrieked.

"Where?"

"On Barrows Island."

Wade's eyes were beginning to bulge, the popping capillaries webbing the whites with red. "Let him go," she pleaded.

"Where in the hotel, dammit?"

Wade's hands clawed futilely at the cable around his neck.

"At the registration desk. Where they keep the mail. Marked 'hold for arrival.' Dad mailed it to himself there."

Lenny gave the cord one final tug. Then he ran for the door.

Andrea threw herself sidewise toward Wade and lay there helplessly, bound hand and foot, watching, as Wade clawed at the knot at the back of his neck, trying to loosen it enough to open an airway.

The room went dark, then bright again. Lenny was backing the car away from the canteen, headlights swinging right and left as he veered crazily, in reverse, toward the highway.

Wade worked the knot loose, flung the strangling cable aside, propped himself up on an elbow and noisily drew in great draughts of air. He watched helplessly as the car shot out across the highway and braked just in time to avoid running into the ditch on the opposite side. The car was out of sight for a moment as a tractor trailer heading north cut off Wade's view. Then he saw it again, for the last time, bouncing up onto the highway and swinging into the northbound lane in the wake of the tractor trailer.

Wade began to undo the cords around Andrea's wrists and

ankles, and then he helped her to her feet. He put his arms around her and held her close. He felt her suddenly go rigid. She uttered a little cry and began slipping away from him. She was down on her knees again, doubled over, clutching at her belly.

Chapter 33

She felt a hand on her forehead, and then it was gone. Then there were fingers pressing against the side of her neck under her jawbone.

A man's voice. Distant, disengaged. "Temperature and pulse seem normal."

"Lloyd?" Her tongue felt thick and unmanageable. They must have dosed her with something to knock her out.

The man's voice: "I'd better have a look inside. Wake her up."

A hand on her shoulder, gently firm. A woman's voice: "Wake up, Miss Tobin. Dr. Scott is here."

Her eyelids felt like lead. She overcame her lassitude and managed to raise them halfway, enough to see the heavily spectacled young man peering down at her. Hawk nose, jutting chin, inquisitive gray eyes. A freshly scrubbed look. Hairy arms growing out of the short sleeves of

231

a freshly laundered white tunic. He looked like a barber.

He began folding her blankets back. "I'm just going to take a look and make sure everything's okay."

"What time is it?" she asked groggily. It was dark outside.

The nurse, dyed blonde and seam-bursting plump, said, "5:30."

"Morning?"

"Evening."

"Where's Lloyd?"

"The gentleman who came in with you?"

Andrea nodded.

"He left."

"Left?" She felt as if she had been cut adrift. She hadn't realized how much she had counted on his being there. "When?"

"About ten this morning, after the doctor assured him you'd be all right."

Well, she thought, at least he'd waited that long. Why should he hang around? The episode was over. Lenny had the file. Lloyd was no longer bound by his promise to help her. The important thing was to take it away from Lenny, even if that meant turning it over to Hull. She had no right to expect any more. But, she had . . . expected. She stared at the ceiling while the doctor poked and peered, humming as he worked.

At last he rolled the blankets up over her again. "You can go home in the morning."

She nodded. And she wondered, where was home?

"Will your friend be coming back for you?" the doctor asked.

Andrea shook her head no.

"We'll have to issue a crutch. You won't be able to walk on that ankle for a while. You can sit up now."

She started to pull herself into a sitting position. The nurse moved to help. "Let her do it herself," the doctor advised.

She was sitting, back against the iron head of the bed. "I'll be all right."

The doctor crossed his hairy forearms across his chest and stood studying her. Then he asked soberly: "You knew you were pregnant, didn't you?"

She nodded. "Were?"

"Yes."

"I'm not anymore?"

"I'm sorry. But maybe it's for the best. You aren't married, are you?" There was no overtone of censure in his question. Nevertheless it hurt her, momentarily, and then she accepted it. Maybe it was for the best.

"Is the guy who brought you in the father?"

"Lloyd? No." She smiled wryly.

The doctor scribbled something on the chart, asked the nurse to see to it that Andrea had some dinner. "I'll be in again to see you in the morning. You can check out anytime before ten o'clock. But make sure you leave before ten, or they'll charge you for another day."

"Thank you."

He nodded and left the room.

She was alone in the room, finishing up her dinner, when there was a knock at the door.

"Come in."

Lloyd hesitated in the doorway for a moment. He was wearing his overcoat, and despite the fact that his cheeks

233

were flushed bright pink from the cold outside, he looked grim and tired. But he was there. Andrea had to make a real effort to hold her emotions in check. She didn't want to start blubbering now.

"Hi there, friend," she said. "I didn't expect to see you again."

"How do you feel?" he asked.

"Fine."

"You look fine."

And she did. She bore no visible scars from her experience of the night before. But she could see, as Lloyd approached, the angry red welt around his throat where the electric cord had been.

He dropped down into the chair beside her bed, a slack, dejected figure, overcoat hanging open, arms hanging limp. "Your brother's gone," he said.

"With the file?" she asked apprehensively.

Wade shook his head wearily. "He didn't wait for the ferry. He stole an outboard dinghy. Nine miles across the sound in a choppy winter sea. A guy who knew anything about boat handling wouldn't have tried it. I think all your brother knew was how to pull the starter cord. He didn't get more than a hundred yards past the breakwater at Gunther Point. They found the dinghy floating upside down a little after sunrise. They found his body on the rocks a few miles below the point this afternoon."

Andrea received the news stolidly. Her fingers idly folded and refolded the hem of the sheet. "I don't feel anything," she said incredulously, "except relief. Does that sound awful?"

"It sounds honest."

She nodded, grateful for Lloyd's understanding. She started

to say something, then hesitated, almost ashamed to give voice to the question that was uppermost in her mind. "Did you go to the island?" she finally asked.

"Yes." He sounded ineffably weary. "The file wasn't there."

Andrea stared at him, dumb with astonishment. "What do you mean, it wasn't there?"

"It wasn't there," he repeated dejectedly. "It never had been there."

Andrea sank back against the pillows. Wade looked up at her with anguished, red-rimmed eyes. "The damned hotel wasn't there." It sounded like an outcry against some unspeakable injustice.

"I don't understand." Her voice was barely audible.

"The family who owned it gave up at the end of last summer. The place was abandoned. Some college kids broke in and roosted there during the Thanksgiving holiday. They were careless. It burned to the ground."

"But my father sent the file there *after* Thanksgiving."

"He didn't know."

"Then where's the file?"

Wade sighed heavily. "I've been thinking about just that for a good part of the afternoon." He stretched out his legs and appeared to become absorbed in the study of his mud-caked shoes. He seemed spent, distracted. Andrea waited patiently. Finally, he fixed her with a quizzical look. "Tell me, Andrea," he asked, squinting against the light from the bedside lamp, his features slightly askew, "do you believe in a hereafter?"

Andrea looked at him with some concern. "What has that got to do with anything?"

"A whole lot, if my guess is right. Because, if there is a hereafter, your father must be laughing his head off right

235

now. Here we've been breaking one another's heads to get hold of those files, and we never really had a chance." He shook a frostbitten finger at her. "Your old man outfoxed us all. And the zinger is, he didn't even know what he had going for him."

Chapter
34

In suite 900 in Jefferson Memorial Hospital, attendants were busy preparing Sewell Crockett for his return home. Crockett was in manic spirits, swinging between jubilation over his release and moroseness over his future.

For the past week the newspapers had been rife with speculation about his imminent retirement. Crockett's doctor had taken the precaution of banning them from the vicinity of his room. But Crockett was not a man who accepted isolation with equanimity. At his direction his private secretary, Miss Yarborough, daily smuggled in a copy of the Washington *Post.* The indications that the President intended to retire him were disheartening. A meretricious statement had been released to the effect that the President was deeply concerned for the health and welfare of a selflessly dedicated public servant. For the first time in his long career, Crockett found himself at a loss. With his file gone he lacked the wherewithal for negotiation.

Two husky orderlies supervised by his nurse and his doctor lowered him into his wheelchair and began tucking a blanket in tightly around his lower extremities.

"Don't make it so snug I can't get my right hand out. I want to be able to wave to the newsboys when those camera lights go on." His speech was unimpaired, but his left side, from shoulder to ankle, was useless.

"You can still change your mind, Sewell," his doctor recommended.

"What? And have them broadcasting all up and down the land that I was in such lousy shape you had to sneak me out a back door so no one would see? Now wouldn't those bastards just love that. Hell, no! I'll give a big wave with the good right arm and a nice sampling of the old Crockett tongue just to show 'em I still have all my marbles, while you roll me past them into the van. You can roll me right in, can't you? I don't want to be lifted out of the chair like a Goddamn cripple."

"There'll be a ramp there, Sewell."

"Good."

"The therapy equipment is already installed at the house."

"And the therapist?"

"He moved in last night. The medical briefing for the press will simply say you've made a good recovery and been discharged. You should be back at your desk after a few weeks' rest and recuperation at home."

Crockett fixed the doctor with a wry look. "You seem to be more optimistic about my health and welfare than our esteemed President."

The doctor frowned, exasperated. "Who's been bringing you newspapers?"

"None of your damned business."

The doctor shook a remonstrating finger at him. "Sewell, for once in your life you've got to follow orders, or you're going to be in serious trouble."

Crockett snorted. He was in serious trouble already, with that damned file loose like a fumbled football and half the world probably scrambling to recover it. If he didn't get it back, that would be the ball game. Goddamn Tobin, anyway. To take that stuff and run with it, and then get himself killed.

"Sewell," the doctor said with concern, "whatever you're thinking, forget it. You're getting red in the face."

"Oh, Christ! Let's get the hell out of here."

They rolled him down the hall to the waiting elevator, then through the improvised press gallery in the lobby, floodlit like a movie set, cameras whirring, microphone stalks thrust in his face. The good right arm held triumphantly aloft. The voice booming out affirmatively regardless of the question. "Never felt better. Lick my weight in wildcats." And then up the ramp, and the door of the van shutting them out.

He sagged in the chair. Goddamn Tobin, anyway. The one man in the world he thought he could trust. Just goes to show. Trust *nobody* . . . ever.

There was a pack of them waiting in his driveway. He knew there would be. The same outthrust microphones. The same non sequitur answers. But he knew that the effect would be just right. When the scene showed up on the home screens that night, the public would see a robust figure waving triumphantly, being wheeled through the crowd like a returning monarch.

Then the door to his house was shut and he sagged again.

His doctor and the therapist wheeled him into the bedroom that had been set up on the first floor. As they passed through the door, he could see in an adjoining room the aluminum walkers and pulleys and weights. He shuddered.

The doctor and the therapist helped him into his bed.

"You'll begin work tomorrow," the doctor said.

"Sure," Crockett said. He was exhausted. "What time is it?"

"11:30."

"I feel like I've been up all day." He was very depressed.

"You've been a sick man, Sewell. Maybe now you'll believe me. Forget the agency for a few weeks."

"Forget my life?"

"For a little while."

"I think I'll take a nap."

"Good idea. I'll see that some lunch is ready for you when you wake up. Then take it easy until tomorrow."

"Maybe I'll do that, Doc."

When he woke up two hours later, Miss Yarborough was sitting beside his bed, smiling in her reserved way. A sparrowlike, white-haired woman, she had served him efficiently and worshipfully for twenty-three years.

"Good afternoon, Mr. Crockett. It's good to have you home." She had meticulously cared for the house while he had been away, paying the bills, cataloguing the mail, fending off reporters. The ultimate measure of her devotion had been the smuggling activity she had recently undertaken in his behalf. At first she had been terrified. The thought of defying authority, especially the sacrosanct authority of a doctor, was foreign to her nature. But Crockett had wanted news. Surprisingly, as the week progressed, she began to find the conspiratorial nature of her mission titillating. Toward

the end, as she negotiated the hospital corridors with a copy
of the *Post* tucked under her coat, and passed the guard at
Crockett's door, she experienced the elation of a gunrunner
successfully slipping through a border checkpoint. She had
never felt closer to Crockett.

"What time is it, Miss Yarborough?"

"Two o'clock."

"Thanks for handling . . . everything."

"I considered it a privilege. Shall I have your lunch brought
in?"

"I haven't had anything decent to drink in two weeks."

"I'm afraid you can't today, either. Doctor's orders."

"Doctor's orders!" Crockett snorted.

Miss Yarborough started to go. Halfway to the door, she
stopped. She stood in the middle of the room, looking ill at
ease and uncharacteristically indecisive.

"What is it, Miss Y.?"

Miss Yarborough nibbled at her lower lip. "The doctor also
said that you weren't to be burdened . . . "

"And you've got something on your mind?"

"Yes, sir."

"Is it important?"

"I think it may be," she said hesitantly. "Otherwise I
wouldn't . . . "

"Then screw the doctor."

Miss Yarborough blanched. Then, her sense of decorum
eroded by her recent adventure, she managed a timorous
smile. "Yes, sir," she said affirmatively. "I'll be right back."

Half a minute later she returned carrying a heavy piece of
mail. "This arrived with today's bundle." She held out the
large, white envelope. "It appears that you mailed it to Mr.
Tobin but that he never received it before he . . . "

241

Crockett looked puzzled. "I sent no mail to Mr. Tobin."

"Then I don't understand . . . " She carefully laid the envelope down on the counterpane for Crockett to see. Crockett looked perplexed. Unquestionably it was stationery from his private stock. His return address was engraved in the upper left-hand corner. But the mailing address scrawled across the face was in Tobin's hand: "Austin Tobin, Sea Cliff Hotel, Barrows Island, Mass." And then, below that, in bold block letters: "HOLD FOR ARRIVAL." The envelope had been around; it was mottled with post office department routing stamps of various sizes and colors. The dominant one, in red ink, read: "RETURN TO SENDER. ADDRESS NONEXISTENT."

Crockett turned the envelope over. The seal appeared to be intact. He looked up at Miss Yarborough, who had stepped back a few respectful paces. "You didn't open it, Miss Y.?"

"No, sir. I didn't think it would be proper. Since it didn't go out through my office, I assumed it was confidential. That's why I felt obliged to bring it to your attention today."

"Thank you, Miss Yarborough."

She recognized the tone of dismissal. "I'll be at my desk if you need me," she said, and left the room.

Crockett waited until she had closed the door. Then he held the envelope up in his good right hand and tore the flap off with his teeth. He spilled the contents out onto his lap and stared down in disbelief.

In her office across the hall Miss Yarborough heard Crockett laughing. He laughed so long and so hard that she became alarmed. She was about to go to his room to investigate when she heard him shout her name. She rushed to his door and threw it open.

Crockett was sitting up in bed, frighteningly red of face. He was wiping tears away from his eyes with the back of his good hand. "Are you all right?" Miss Yarborough cried out. "Shall I call the doctor?"

"Hell, no!" Crockett jubilantly roared. "I want you to call the White House. The President and I have matters of mutual interest to discuss."

Miss Yarborough brightened. "Right away, sir."

"And then I want my lunch . . . *with* bourbon and water."

Miss Yarborough looked dubious.

"Well, I'll be damned if I'll drink to Tobin's ghost with grapefruit juice."

"Yes, sir," Miss Yarborough exclaimed, losing herself in the spirit of the moment. "And screw the doctor?"

"Screw them all, Miss Y. Screw them all!" With that final, triumphant pronouncement, Sewell Crockett fell over, dead.

Epilogue

Sewell Crockett was buried at Arlington with the highest honors the nation could bestow, while much of Washington officialdom quietly breathed a sigh of relief. The newspaper editorial writers, who had spent the better part of a week according Crockett's career mixed reviews, began to turn their attention to the primary battle looming between General Wilton Dahlgren and Senator John Ashley, both of whom hoped to be the next president of the United States.

Miss Yarborough, secluded in her efficiency apartment on Q Street, felt rootless and bereft, almost as if she were a bona fide widow. Like many widows, she felt a little bit betrayed and guiltily concerned about the problems of survival. The years that were left to her looked bleak. Her savings were meager, and she could expect no pension, for she had not been a civil service employee. After all her years of devoted service she might have hoped to be remembered in Crockett's will, had he remembered to make one. But he had believed until the last in his immortality.

She wished that she could just vanish, book passage on one of the luxury ships that spend the winter months on 'round-the-world cruises, and disappear. "See the world before you leave it," the advertisements urged. She had never really seen anything, never been anywhere.

Sighing, she opened the envelope that she had removed from Crockett's bedroom for safekeeping on the afternoon that he had died. Carefully she laid out what remained of the contents on her kitchen table. Days ago she had destroyed the set of keys that had been taped to the cardboard inside. She had suspected what they were for and had been concerned about the mischief they might cause if they fell into the wrong hands. But she had kept the tape cassette and the transcript that Crockett must have typed himself. She had, until now, been reluctant to admit to herself the reason why. But after days of agonized soul-searching she had finally concluded that there was a limit to selflessness; one had a right to survive. One had to make do with the resources at hand.

Senator Ashley would certainly be interested in the transcript and the tape. General Dahlgren might be interested, too. And the President. Perhaps the best thing to do would be to contact all the concerned parties, anonymously, of course, and invite bids.

She remembered Crockett's last words and thought that he would approve.

245

00686 2875

$c_i 2$

Green
See how they run.